C000152221

Published by Stuart Kenyon 2019

Stuart Kenyon asserts the moral right to be identified as the
author of this work.

For Vicky, Max and Poppy

Chapter 26 — Luke Norman — 04:00

Luke holds Connor close. "We didn't get far enough!"

"We did," Gould insists. "Just get your heads down."

They obey, and not a moment too soon. A nearby boom rocks the bus. One of the windows shatters, showering the passengers with chunks of jagged plastic. The children and Ashara squeal in panic, but they're swiftly silenced as the driver executes a ninety degree turn.

When the back of the bus clips a blazing coach, Jada is thrown from her seat. The fall saves her life, though; an explosion launches an object through the glass of the emergency door.

Evie's not so lucky. The flying wing mirror catches her flush in the face with a nauseating thud.

Sobbing, Connor lurches towards her, but he's pulled back when Gould takes evasive action as the latest missile craters the dual carriageway ahead. "Hold on!" he yells. Somehow, he manages to squeeze the single-decker through a gap in the central reservation.

Luke drags his son away from the bloody-faced girl across the aisle. "Stay with me!" he barks over the sound of screeching tyres. The boy's shaking in his arms now, clinging to his father like a toddler.

Again the brakes are slammed. Just in time, Luke's right hand shoots out to the bench in front, preventing him from crushing Connor against it.

Please just stop, Luke silently begs. *Mortborough can't be more than a pile o' rubble now. This is overkill.*

"Nearly clear now." Gould's voice is disconcertingly placid as he manoeuvres around the jack-knifed oil tanker that caused him to halt.

Everyone takes a deep breath. There have been no detonations for —

The fuel truck blows up in slow motion. Instantly engulfed in flame, the bus bounces away as if backhanded by a giant. The passengers screech as they are immolated. Apart from Joshua Gould, who roars with laughter…

…And now they're trapped. The bus's doors are sealed shut, and the vehicle is surrounded by zombies. Strong, dead fingers are prying at the windows. Fists pound on the windscreen. The undead all have faces Luke recognises: his father, Christopher Norman; his ex, Connor's mother; Jada Blakowska, her beautiful face contorted by spite…

He wakes with a half-gasp, half-whimper that stirs Jada without waking her. For a moment he panics: he checks his hands and legs, but there's no sign of any burning. There's nobody banging on the bus's sides, either. The sound was part of his nightmare, and now it's gone.

We did *escape Mortborough.*

The closest missile struck at least fifty yards to their rear. Though terrifying, the bombardment did them no physical harm. Apart from the tinnitus Luke incorrectly presumed would be gone by the time he woke. Shaking his head doesn't help; in fact, the movement only serves to aggravate a stiff neck, one of the many injuries he incurred yesterday.

Groaning, Luke sits up on the bus's back bench. The sky is still black with night, though the burning warehouse across the road from Walkley's shopping mall lends its own illumination. Raindrops are on the pane, but the clouds are clearing now. His own trembling, pale hand, resting on the windowsill, catches his attention. The knuckles are skinned, the fingertips filthy. It reminds him of the zombies' grasping paws.

Reality hits him like a sledgehammer. *My town is dead. My 'ome town completely destroyed.* In the space of fourteen hours, Mortborough, Greater Manchester, went from leafy suburb to warzone, with a short stint as land of the living dead in the middle. *Zombies. Fuckin' zombies.*

But if complete annihilation was what the town needed to stop the undead apocalypse in its tracks, it would be a price worth paying. Twenty thousand would be dead. Better that, however, than a plague which consumed the whole of the UK.

What if there'd been another way, though? 'N' what if the infection's already spread, 'n' the missiles were fer nothin'?

One man thought so. During the short drive from Mortborough to Walkley, before the supposedly-repaired bus surrendered, Josh Gould made his feelings very clear. The Government, or the military, or whoever, took the nuclear option – figuratively speaking – far too readily. Connor's and Evie's mums could've been saved. Now they would be nothing but broken, barbecued bodies.

He hadn't wanted to say as much to the bereft youngsters before they went to sleep, though, in retrospect, such bluntness may have prevented at least an hour of bickering. Pure chance meant they were passing the motorway turn-off for the Crawford Centre shopping complex when the PCV's engine began to fail. An argument ensued when Connor Norman and Evie Callaghan decided they were going to venture out of the stalled vehicle and head back to Mortborough to search for their respective mothers.

Stupid, brave little shits.

Luke doesn't remember much thereafter. Exhausted beyond comprehension, he'd dismissed the kids' plans and told them to get some rest.

The last thing he recalls before losing consciousness is a debate between Brad and Gould. The former, still flitting between silent despair over executing his own zombified daughter and a burning, energising compulsion to hold someone accountable, was in fight mode. Like Connor and Evie, he was determined to return to their hometown. Evidence of government/Evolve shenanigans was there, waiting to be discovered and publicised. The bus station manager didn't dispute his conviction. But, in his opinion, seeking said proof was suicidal. The powers-that-be launched an indiscriminate missile strike to keep their secret. They were willing to accept any collateral damage to protect their interests. Now the warring pair slumber; no doubt they'll be at each other's throats again in the morning.

Although Jada was more circumspect, she too wanted to expose those responsible for yesterday. She was content, however, to sleep on the decision. Her soft snores continue to sound from the seat in front of Luke.

Ashara was far from reticent during the discussion. Her priority was survival, which, she believed, was best secured by staying with the group. Of course, it would help if the group steered clear of the undead, but she was sufficiently shrewd to recognise that, as the gang's newest member, she wouldn't be calling the shots.

And what about Luke? Now that he's saved Connor, he feels purposeless. Perhaps his torpor is simply a symptom of PTSD; maybe he needs more rest, more time to come to terms with the end of his world as he knew it.

You dick. There's no time for rest. No time for feelin' sorry fer yerself. Need t' get t' Dad, Maddie 'n' Mason in Atherbury; get outta the city, away from the monsters 'n' bombs.

Rescuing his son was just the start, and now he needs to keep the boy out of harm's way. With that in mind, he rises slowly to his feet to check on Connor and Evie. He blinks dumbly when he sees the vacant seats they occupied.

What. The. Fuck.

The father chides himself, for they've probably just gone outside to urinate. Their doing so likely woke him, not bad dreams. Even so, hard logic can't quell the chill ascending his spine. He takes a few deep breaths to steady himself, his nose wrinkling at the smell of stale bodies.

Taking care, in the gloom, not to brush against any of the feet protruding into the bus's central aisle, he moves towards the front of the vehicle. His route takes him no closer than six feet to Gould.

Propped up in the driver seat, the former transport supervisor wakes; almost comically, his right eye opens while the left stays shut. "What are you doing?" the older man asks.

"Connor. Evie." Luke lips his lips. "They're not 'ere."

"We told them to go outside if they need a piss."

"Yeah."

"So that's probably it. They've gone outside for a piss. Must've been quiet, though. I'm a very light sleeper."

"I noticed. They'd be back by now, though, wouldn't they? If they were just goin' fer a piss, I mean."

"Maybe one o' them needs a shit."

"Hmm. Gonna go take a look outside."

"Sure. Give me a shout if you need me."

Luke's hand shakes as he reaches for the exit button. *Somethin's not right.* The door opens, and the night's breeze is cool on his clammy brow. The smell of burning plastic is in the air. Falteringly, he alights onto the pavement, squinting against the Vegas-style neon "Crawford Centre" sign affixed to a department store's wall.

Behind him, the bus's doors hiss closed, and an airliner drones high above. But another sound has him spinning on his heel. It's a noise he heard for the first time yesterday, and it can only signify one thing. Wet jaws, opening and closing; a gasp, not a breath, a mockery of human respiration.

There's no one around, though, so perhaps his mind's playing tricks on him. *Focus, dickhead.* He needs to find Connor before the little pest gets himself into trouble. Circling the single-decker, he mutters curses to himself. The two children shouldn't be wandering off on their own, but he ought to have told them as much before he passed out earlier. If something's happened to them —

There it is again, unmistakable this time: a zombie is nearby. Standing still, with his back against the bus and his heart thrumming in his ears, he looks left and right. "Gould," he calls.

Within seconds, the driver is at the bus's doors. "Trouble?"

"Shh. Just listen."

"To what. I can't —" Gould head jerks to one side, like a deer scenting predators. He puts a hand to the mammoth revolver tucked into his belt. "It's on top of the bus."

Feeling naked without a weapon, Luke takes a step forward. Then another. After a third, he twists. There's nothing there. "You sure?" he breathes.

Gould continues to stare at the vehicle roof as he backs away. Drawing his handgun, he nods. "Definitely. Heard a bump before I jumped out, but thought it was a bird." He aims upwards with one hand, wipes sweat from his brow with the other. His gun arm is steady, his jaw muscles tight.

'I'll shout the others. More firepower."

"No. We need to do this quietly. There might be more nearby —" Gould is silenced by a soft thud on the other side of the bus. He puts a finger to his lips. "The silenced Glock," he whispers. "Get it."

As Gould slowly backsteps away, Luke climbs back aboard the bus and fetches the gun in question.

Brad stirs. "What's up?"

"Zombie." Luke tips his head towards the doors.

His friend rouses himself swiftly and grabs the Sig Sauer pistol. Within seconds, all three of the men are in the open, their gaze intent on the tarmac either side of the PCV.

"We need to get rid of it, quick. Before more come." Gould points his Enfield in the direction of the still-afire warehouse across the road. "Let's lead them that way. The fire'll help us see them. And it'll buy me time to get everyone off the bus."

"Then we find the kids," Luke adds.

"Right. I'm quickest," says Brad. "I'll lure 'em."

"Okay." Gould holds one forefinger aloft, as if he's a teacher. "But Brad, don't open fire unless you absolutely need to. Let's try and do this as quietly as possible."

Brad breaks away from the others, heading towards the smouldering building.

Immediately, a dark figure lurches from behind the bus. Arms outstretched, the tracksuit-wearing dead man walks spasmodically, like an old clockwork toy.

Squinting, Luke draws a bead on the zombie with the suppressed Glock. It's twelve yards away.

"Just take it down," Gould urges. "Then you can get closer and headshot it. I'll start waking everyone up."

Luke squeezes off three rounds. Two fly true, hitting the freak's left hip and knee. Emitting a sound like tearing Velcro, it goes down and begins to crawl towards Brad, who's standing, hands on hips, with his back to the burning warehouse.

Now Luke jogs over to his downed foe, while Gould goes in the other direction, around the back of the bus. The younger man aims the handgun at the freak's blood-spattered shaven head. Just as he's about to fire, the abomination registers his proximity and turns to face him.

Fuck me. 'Ow does it manage t' turn its neck like that? Like it's dislocated, or something —

"Luke!" Brad yells. "Watch out!"

There's another zombie. This one *underneath* the bus, not on its roof. And it's on top of Luke before he can react. He goes down. Lands heavily, but he just about gets a grip of the thing's greasy hair before its snaggletoothed maw gets too close. A blood-soaked necktie is dangling in his face, the tip tickling his lips. The stench of sour milk and faeces envelops Luke, making him want to gag. Footsteps nearby: Brad coming to help. Scream from Ashara. Jada panicking.

His left arm is weakening. His right scrabbling on the tarmac as he strives to reach the Glock. *Just another few inches…*

But also, just another few inches before the monster eats his face. "Fire, Brad! Fer fucksake, fire!"

The Sig cracks a reply; the fiend shudders and slumps.

Luke twists his head to avoid taking a mouthful of brain matter. "Ugh!" He shoves the twice-dead man away and gets to his feet.

The pop of the Glock makes him jump, but it's only Gould, dispatching the crippled, crawling zombie before it can grip Luke's ankle.

Putting a hand on his shoulder, Jada says, "Are you alright, Luke?"

"Yeah, thanks." He wipes undead blood from his ear. "But we need to find Connor and Evie."

"Quickly, too." Gould is staring northwards, at the Crawford Centre's main entrance. "Somehow, I doubt the zombs we just killed are the only ones in the area."

Chapter 27 — Theo Callaghan — 04:30

Squeezing his eyes shut makes no difference.

He needs a brain wipe, a factory reset of his mind. To clear his mental cache of all the x-rated filth he's downloaded in the last twelve or so hours. Like in those books he's been reading, where people's minds are implanted with computers that allow the user full control over their memories. Failing that, since he's not in the 2060s, there must be drugs that can help him forget.

Idiot. Even if there are drugs like that, who's gonna prescribe 'em? Zombie doctors?

So, no sleep it is. Theo's beyond fatigued, but every time he lays his head to rest on the bin bag full of cushions, every time he lets his gritty eyelids close, the monsters return. Rendered in 4K resolution, the gore-soiled abominations menace him almost as vividly as they did yesterday. He can no longer imagine his father's face as it was on Sunday or Saturday. Only as it was on Monday: grey-skinned, bloodshot-eyed, split-lipped, nose half-bitten off, teeth gummed with his fiancée's flesh and hair.

The thirteen year-old boy cuffs a single tear from his cheek. *At least* I'm *alive. Thank Mary, Mother o' God for that, as Granny Trisha used to say.*

Plus, Theo's about as safe as he can be at the moment. He's in the wine cellar beneath one of the grand, old townhouses overlooking Walkley Park. It's the sort of place Dad used to say they would inhabit when his twenty year mobile DJ career took off. In fact, they walked down this very road hand-in-hand many a time when Theo was younger, when Evie was a toddler riding her dad's shoulders. Mum used to chuckle to herself, cynically.

Patrick Callaghan's kept his promise this time, though, for his heir has inherited 22 Thornhaven Drive lock, stock and barrel. Its former owners are dead or undead. This is Theo's house now. For the time being, he's restricted to its basement, but at some point, the armed forces will come and blast the undead invaders to kingdom come. Because that's what the British Army do. They protect the vulnerable and destroy the wicked. One day, Theo will return the favour by enlisting himself. He'll fight in the next war against the living dead, and he'll be the heroic soldier saving children and shooting zombies.

Fucksake, Theo. Get a grip. Ya might not even make it through this *war, the way things are goin'.*

"Yeah, I will. Just need t' sit tight 'n' wait it out. The Army'll come, 'n' I'll be saved."

He stands. Full of nervous energy, yet weak with tiredness, he paces the hard concrete floor. It smells damp down here, like wet washing left too long. The lightbulb is naked and bright, casting shadows of wine boxes and ancient furniture on the bare brick walls. Though hungry, Theo feels nauseous. He's thirsty, and the only drink available is alcoholic. Sitting and resting would be wiser, but he needs to occupy his thoughts. Unguarded, they stray back to the previous day.

At about 4pm, Betty the tabby cat went feral and attacked her former friend/sparring partner, Colin the Cocker Spaniel. She tore out the poor mutt's throat, turning him into a zombie dog in turn. Dad killed both of their pets with a shovel, only to succumb to the postman in the hallway of their semi-detached. Theo fled upstairs and locked himself in the bathroom, the door of which his father battered till his girlfriend, Sophie, arrived. Screaming, banging and tearing sounds followed, then silence. Darkness had fallen by the time the boy found the courage to escape, and he did so by the skin of his teeth. He was chased by Dad-zombie for two streets before easier pickings – a lost, probably orphaned infant on Hardaker Road – drew the late Mr Callaghan's attention.

Therefore, as well as dealing with the trauma of his world being drowned in blood, the young man is burdened with a guilty conscience. He could've intercepted Sophie, the stepmother-to-be he disdained at first yet grew to like, before she got to his house. He could've warned her about her partner's transformation. But he didn't, and now she's dead. Just like the little girl on Hardaker that Dad devoured instead of Theo. He didn't deserve to find this safe haven, with its door wide open, its occupants slaughtered but still to turn, its cellar unlocked.

But it is what it is, bro. You survived. They didn't.

What next, then? While he might not get caught by zombies down here, he won't last long without food and water. And although seeking sustenance will be perilous, perhaps he can find other survivors. Dad's gone. This reality rakes at his soul, makes him feel nauseous and faint and raw, as if he's been exposed to radiation. But he has other loved ones. His younger sister, Evie, lives in Mortborough with their mum. There's Gabriela Popescu as well, Theo's best friend and secret crush, who also lives in Walkley, half a mile from the park.

If not already dead, all three females could be in danger. Theo must try to help them. He's not sexist, unlike some of his friends, but these are primitive times. It's kill or be killed now. He's nearly a man, so he needs to act like one. First, he'll go to Gabriela's tower block; then, once he's rescued her, he can make the short trip to Mortborough to search for his mother and sister.

That's if you've got the balls t' go outside. Ya didn't even show up fer the fight with Devon Atkinson last week, so 'ow ya gonna face those flesh-munchin' freaks outside, eh?

He'll take a weapon. No, he'll get two: one heavy and blunt; the other sharp. There's been no movement in the house above him for over an hour now, so he should have enough time to find something suitably lethal before he leaves.

Jaw set, Theo crosses the basement floor. His legs become more leaden with every step he takes. At the bottom of the stairs, he runs out of steam. Suddenly, he's hyperventilating, his vision swimming; he has to steady himself on the handrail. "Come on, Theo. You can do this. Yer *not* scared. Just go up the stairs, find some food 'n' weapons, 'n' dust."

Evie used to laugh at him for talking to himself, but, somehow, he finds comfort in hearing a voice. After taking a puff on his new inhaler, he begins his ascent. He treads slowly, partly due to fear, mostly to be quiet.

The cellar key is still in the lock on Theo's side. He turns it slowly, ears straining for any sign he's been heard. Thankfully, the hinges are well-oiled, so there's no sound as he pushes the door wide. Broad and long, the house's main hallway is modern in decoration, with little in the way of furniture. As well as the imposing front entrance, which faces a stairwell, and the one he's just come through, there are four doors. The rearmost is ajar, and he can see silver appliances, a refrigerator and freezer.

Still listening intently, Theo creeps into the kitchen. It's a substantial space, at least twice the size of Mum's or Dad's. A table is knocked over, as are two chairs, but apart from that, there's no sign of any disturbance. He opens the fridge, drinks a litre of apple juice and wolfs down a packet of honey-roast ham and a slice of cheesecake.

Now for the front door. The day's first light is visible through the frosted glass either side of the wooden frame. Fingers dancing, he reaches for the handle —

Feathers flutter. Theo turns, heart in mouth, as a large squirrel appears from the stairway. The rodent lands on the bannister, cocks its head to one side and eyeballs the boy. A single drop of blood falls from its mouth.

Abandoning stealth, the teen flees 22 Thornhaven, slamming the door behind himself in a panic. While the street outside is desolate, evidence of the ongoing chaos is ample. He can smell burning, as though autumn is in the air. Cars are crashed into one another. Smoke's on the horizon. Under an anorexic tree, there are two corpses.

Looking away from the dead man and woman, Theo wonders why some victims become zombies moments or hours after death, but others simply die. *Would I turn? 'N' if I did, would I even know what was goin' on?*

He shakes his head. "C'mon, dickhead. Time t' go."

His route to the Orion flats will lead him near his school. It'll take him a little longer, but he consciously avoids Parker Road, because that's where his life changed forever. Or, at least, that's where he realised his life was changing forever. A little after three o'clock, yesterday, as he was on his way home from Walkley High, a wild-looking woman dove in front of a car travelling at about 30mp/h.

Theo can still hear the thud if he closes his eyes. Cursed by an eidetic memory, he can picture the woman flying through the air, landing on the tarmac, then crawling back towards the saloon that hit her, the driver jumping out of his car and going to help, only to be dragged to the ground…

"Focus, Theo!"

He takes a left, then two rights. Save for a timid cat and a few birds, he sees no signs of life. He does, however, hear a cry from one of the terraced houses he passes on Dijonnaise Street. Plus, further away, a series of crackles like fireworks. *Gunfire. It's the Army! They'll sort this shit out.*

The next turn leaves him on Mortborough Road, a wider thoroughfare lined with skeletal trees. Seeing their withering branches usually makes Theo glum, but not today. Because he can also see the closest twenty-storey apartment block, North Star House, just one hundred yards away. Gabriela lives in Great Bear House, which is close by.

He could head straight down Mortborough Road. Instead, he'll use the back alley running parallel with the main road, so that he doesn't have to walk past the row of shops, most of which have ominously-open doors. Turning into the ginnel, he disturbs a bunch of crows. They leave the bloodied body of an obese child for a moment, but they return to their meal as soon as Theo's hurried past.

At the end of the alleyway, he has to step around another carcass. The jet-skinned man shifts as the boy splashes through a puddle. *Shit!* Head down, Theo sprints across Memorial Street, hurdles a crash barrier and slips through a gate in the fence around the towers. He ducks behind a bin then risks a look to his rear.

The dead man is now on its feet and is shambling in Theo's direction.

If I can just get t' the closest tower...

He stands; the zombie's step quickens; the boy runs.

Skidding to a stop at the closed main entrance to North Star, he mashes the intercom buttons, alerting as many of the apartments as he can. There's no response. And the walking corpse is getting closer, stumbling into the trash can behind which Theo hid.

"C'mon!" He presses more switches, his only reward the beep of unanswered buzzes.

Now there's another sound. Up in the sky, there's a massive aeroplane, but that's not what Theo heard. Maybe thirty feet off the ground, a mini-helicopter emerges from behind North Star House. Briefly it hovers, before a cylinder attached to its nose flashes white. A machine gun rattles, startling a group of pigeons. The zombie shudders as red flowers appear on its yellow t-shirt, staggers for a moment, then drops to the pavement.

"Yes!" Theo punches the air. "Fuckin' 'ave some o' that, ya bastard!" He almost thanks the drone but settles for a wave.

The UAV remains still, the only sound that of its whirling rotors. Almost imperceptibly, the barrel of its cannon twitches.

Is it aiming at me*? It's aiming at me.* The teenager bursts away just as the gun spits a second stream of lead. Glass shatters. Brickwork is chipped. Keeping his head down, Theo scrambles away.

Chapter 28 — Jada Blakowska — 05:55

"What's the odds this one'll be empty too?" Brad asks as they prepare to enter the latest designer boutique.

"Probably pretty strong," she replies. "But the doors are open, so…"

"I know, I know." Pistol levelled, the diminutive man steps over broken glass.

The shop is shrouded in darkness, the mannequins almost creepy amidst the destruction. Clothes rails are upended. A mirror is cracked and sheeted with dark liquid that pools on the carpet below.

"Wonder 'ow Luke 'n' Gould are doin'?" Brad checks the changing booths.

The other two are searching the cinema, bowling alley, VR arcades and crazy golf course that are nominally part of the Crawford Centre despite being physically separate.

"Dunno." Jada opens a door marked 'RESTRICTED TO STAFF' to find an office not much bigger than a closet. "That's the problem. We've no way of contacting them if we get lucky, and vice versa. And Ashara can't tell us if the kids go back to the bus."

"Whole thing's fucked."

"Has been since yesterday. I think we're done here."

They move onto the next unit, a mobile phone retailer. It'll be the twenty-first they've investigated since gaining access to the mall by climbing onto a dumpster then slipping through a toilet window. Jada's ankle, injured yesterday during the tussle with Lunt, is throbbing. She's almost ready to quit.

The phone place is in worse shape than the clothes store next door. Obviously looted, it has none of the usual signs of zombie incursion. No blood, no innards, no vomit. Nor are there any pre-teen children. Jada and Brad sigh in synchrony, which makes them both laugh.

"Stupid kids," the latter says, sitting on a mall bench.

"I know." Jada traipses to a mobile ice cream shop and pilfers two bottles of water from its fridge. She tosses one to Brad and drinks deeply from the other, before taking a seat next to her companion. "Two minute break. Then we'll crack on." Her neck is tense, so she massages it while breathing in through her nose and out of her mouth. Although they've seen little in the way of undead activity – only one corpse in a lingerie chain and a few patches of blood – it smells rotten in here. Perhaps it's spoiling meat or dairy in the various food outlets.

"Fuck, I'm tired," she yawns.

Brad nods. "Me too. D'ya think we'll find 'em?"

"Not sure."

"We can't search forever, though, can we?"

"No. But if we don't find 'em…"

"I know. Luke'll be devastated."

"That Evie, she reminds me of my sister."

"Ya got a sister? Ya never mentioned —"

"*Had* a sister. Hanna. She died when she was seven, and I was twelve."

"Shit." Brad looks at his filthy trainers. "Sorry 'bout that."

She gives him a tight smile then finishes her water. "It was a long time ago. But she went missin', too, on holiday in Spain. She drowned. Accidental, the police said."

"Poor kid."

As they continue their search, Jada dwells on Hanna's death. She was supposed to be watching her sister while their parents went to the shop. Naturally, Mum and Dad didn't hold her accountable; they blamed themselves for shirking responsibility. Still, Jada's always felt guilty. Maybe, if she can ensure Evie comes to no harm, she'll be atoning in some small part for her negligence with Hanna.

They clear three more shops in quick succession, discovering nothing but damaged fixtures, broken glass and a dead female retail worker, whose right arm has been severed. However, Jada does steal a ready-to-use camera from an electronics shop.

Their next destination is the food court, which was a regular haunt for Jada during her adolescence. Searching its myriad restaurants and kiosks is a laborious task, and she feels her resolve ebbing away. She's weary and frazzled. Though ashamed by the sentiment, she's beginning to lose patience with following other people's agendas.

Of course, she does want to find the children. She hates to see Luke so desperate and is chastened by the thought of Connor and Evie fending for themselves. But she also craves justice. Retribution against the government and corporation that unleashed hell on her hometown. Even for an investigative journalist of Jada's calibre, sourcing evidence of their wrongdoing won't be easy. A difficult task will become an impossible one if she doesn't act soon. While she's being led on a wild goose chase by a couple of kids, shadowy forces will be at work, striving to exculpate themselves.

Evolve and Villeneuve can't get away with this. They must *face consequences. This is too big to sweep under the carpet.*

"Penny fer 'em?" Brad says as they leave a fried chicken franchise.

"Eh?" Jada opens a bar and grill's double front doors. "Oh, I'm just pissed off, is all."

"Wi' what? I mean, apart from the obvious, our town bein' torn t' shreds by zombies 'n' missiles, 'n' everythin'."

"Just… I dunno. It's… complicated."

"Ya wanna get 'em back, don't ya? The bastards who caused all o' this."

"Yeah. But it just feels like…"

"Like we're just fightin' t' survive. Like there's no chance o' getting' revenge."

"Yeah."

While Jada checks the ladies' bathroom, Brad does the mens'. "'N' while we're runnin' 'round lookin' for the kids, everythin' else goes on the back-burner, right?"

She winces. "I feel awful even thinkin' it. I mean, Luke's son's missin' for the second time in two days. He must be goin' out of his mind. And I'm bitchin' about not gettin' payback."

"Don't feel bad, girl. Anger's a strong emotion, innit. Shit, I'm angry too."

"I know. What happened to your daughter… it was —"

"— Fuckin' awful. Probably never get over it, will I? But what can I do? There's no time t' process it all right now. There's only two things I can do."

"What?"

"Survive. 'N' 'elp you screw those fuckers over. But Luke's my friend, so I've gotta try 'n' 'elp find his kid."

"I know. Course you do. I wasn't sayin' for a minute that we shouldn't be helpin' him. *I* wanna help him too. But that's not *all* I wanna do."

"For now," Brad begins, stepping around a dead chef in the bar's kitchen, "it's a pretty simple choice."

Jada opens a walk-in freezer and finds only frozen food. "Between lookin' after the livin' and avengin' the dead?"

"Right."

"All about priorities, I guess. But if I do see somethin', somethin' I can tie to the Government, or military, or Evolve, you bet your arse I'll use it."

"Damn right. 'N' I'll be —"

Suddenly, the utensils hanging from hooks are rattling as a boom is accompanied by a couple of seconds' rumbling. Jada and Brad share a look. A second explosion is followed by a third. Dust falls from the ceiling; alarms sound somewhere in the complex.

"That was pretty close," says Jada. "So they're still bombing."

"But not just Mortborough." Brad wipes grit from his hair.

"We'd better finish the food court quick. We're on the west side of the centre here, closest to Mortborough."

The pair rush from takeaway to vendor, clearing the second half of the food court in five minutes. Now on the first floor, they head back into the mall proper.

"Reckon we're about a third o' the way there." Brad leans against a fake palm tree for a moment, seemingly mesmerised by a fountain modelled on an orca. Water, erupting from the marble mammal's blowhole, sparkles in the early morning sun pouring through the glass dome above.

"Ground floor done, food court done. Just the first floor now." Jada nods at the closest shop. "They're mostly bigger units up here, too, so it shouldn't take too long." *But why are we just tryin' to get it over an' done with, like it's a chore? Surely we should be hopin' to find the kids.*

When they reach the first shop on the right, a department store, they stop dead. Behind the multiple doors, there are at least half a dozen zombies.

"Maybe try somewhere else first?" Brad suggests.

"No." Jada snaps a few photographs then hangs her new camera from her neck. "If the kids are in there, they'll need our help."

"I guess." Brad checks his pistol as Jada does likewise with her MP5. "Why the zombies only in here, though?"

"There's a way in from outside, the first floor car park. They must've wandered in."

"C'mon." Tentatively, Jada pushes open one of the glass doors. Submachine gun ready, she enters the store. Brad is close behind. The closest enemy was once a gentleman in his sixties; now it's a crimson-drenched beast missing two fingers from its left hand.

Ammunition's low, so the MP5's set to semi-automatic. Jada puts a hole in the zombie's forehead before it's moved more than a yard. Straightaway, she's aiming and firing at another, a heavily-pregnant Hispanic woman.

Meanwhile, Brad shoots one in a firefighter's uniform. He tucks his handgun in his belt, then stoops to grab the axe the zombie was carrying. "Saving ammo," he barks before burying the tool's blade in a perfume counter rep's bouffanted head.

"You're enjoying that too much," Jada snarks, headshotting a lanky security guard and a female shopper.

"You're projectin'." Brad extricates the axe, which is now sticky with blood and blonde hair.

He's right. I do relish the gore and violence. What kinda person *am I?*

Both high on adrenaline, the duo conduct a fruitless sweep of the shop floor. Brad has to use his new weapon again when a changing room attendant surprises them, but they encounter no further resistance. Before leaving, they close and barricade the entrance that the zombies have been using.

The next ten places yield similar results. A couple of stray monsters are swiftly eliminated, and it appears the gunfire is not attracting any unwanted attention. They grab chocolate, crisps and sodas from a newsagents and refresh themselves on the move.

In fact, as luck would have it, they're almost finished when they find anything of note. At the opposite end to the food court, the Crawford Centre has a premium bicycle shop, a branch of the 'Hot Wheels' chain. It's been raided, one of the windows smashed.

"This blood," Jada points to a jagged shard of glass protruding from the door. "It looks fresh."

"'N' wasn't Evie chewin' gum?" Brad nods at a wad on the floor.

"Yeah. I mean, on their own, they're not the best of clues, but the two bikes that're missin'..." There's a space in the window display big enough to feature two bikes.

Brad reads the model descriptions aloud. "Sounds like a boy's 'n' a girl's."

"I don't know if it's enough to confirm it's definitely them." Jada takes a step back to appraise the scene as a whole. In her peripheral vision, she notices a CCTV camera on the ceiling, just inside the unit. "I guess there's one way to be sure."

Realising what she's thinking, Brad heads for the rear of the shop, with Jada close behind. He uses his axe to smash into the office. Once inside, he gets to work on a computer while she watches for hostiles.

"Shit, password protected."

"Just do your best." *What was that noise?* MP5 at the ready, Jada goes back to Hot Wheels's exit and checks the area immediately outside. It's deserted.

Brad exclaims, "I'm in! Password was the company name, fer fucksake."

Jada glances over her shoulder. "Fast rewind the last couple of hours," she calls.

"No shit, genius."

Four minutes later, he's gesturing for her to come see. "Got 'em. Look. This was… just an hour ago."

"Right." Jada sighs, watching the grainy figures on the screen. On the whole, Connor and Evie aren't distinctive-looking kids, but the latter's rainbow-coloured hair-bow is a give-away. "Best find Luke."

Chapter 29 — Floyd Nelson — 07:05

His first deployment.

'Travel the world', the Army's website trumpeted. 'Experience different cultures'. 'Be the best you can be'.

But Private Nelson's not been sent to some exotic jungle or Middle Eastern caliphate. *Fuckin' shithole.* He's never liked Manchester, not since visiting an uncle up here as a teen. It's too dreary, too cold during the winter. For him, the old Victorian mill he's passing epitomises the industrial north. Crumbling red brick, pools of milky rainwater, dead weeds fluttering in the breeze, graffiti'd garages, dented barrels brown with rust. Even bathed in the early morning sunshine, it's a grim place.

Of course, the South London district in which he was raised is far from perfect. The fact he recently reached his twenty-third birthday without being a victim, perpetrator or witness of knife crime is a testament to his Jamaican mother's firm hand and Christian values.

"Eh, Nelson!" Fellow Grenadier Guardsman, Private Gurdeep Singh, nudges his friend. "Wake up, fam."

"What's up?"

"Nuffin, just, ya know, stay sharp."

"I always was a bit of a daydreamer." He suddenly becomes conscious of the weight of the rifle in his hands. There's a whiff of burning in the air, and something else on the westerly wind; it reminds him of the abattoir that employed his older brother.

"Yeah, well, we're nearly there now. Other side of this mill, serge said."

"Don't you fink it's a bit weird?"

"*What's* a bit weird?"

"Da whole company's 'ere, innit?"

"Yeah."

"An' us two, we're da greenest, ain't we?"

"Yeah, so? What's your point?"

As Floyd emerges from behind the mill's easternmost wall, he sees the Swinford council estate to which they've been sent. It's not like King's Meadow, Croydon. These houses were built in the seventies rather than post-2000; they look tired, though the people within are probably no different to those in South London.

"Floyd?" Gurdeep is waiting on a grass verge overlooking the boggy field between the soldiers and their destination. "You comin', or what? Serge'll 'ave our arses if we don't hustle up."

Floyd shakes his head. "I know, I know." He hurries over to his comrade, who's already climbing over an ancient stone wall. Unlike Gurdeep, he has long legs, so he quickly catches up. Together they tramp across the fen, boots heavy in the mud. "You know what, Gurdeep?"

"No, but ya still ain't told me what's 'weird' about us two, the newest recruits, being 'ere, so I ain't 'oldin' my breath."

"Yer very patient wiv me, Gurdeep. 'Specially 'cause I's a SE13 chief, 'n' you's representin' SE3."

"Nah. I was a good boy, me. I was never involved in all that shit."

"Me neiva, blud. But what I was sayin'," Floyd skirts a particularly deep-looking pool of water, "was it's weird, me 'n' you, bein' sent off on our own like this."

"Hmm." Gurdeep, watching a small aircraft, a drone perhaps, on the western horizon, almost slips in the mire. In profile, with his manly beard and strong nose, the Sikh is a handsome man. *Stop finkin' like dat, Floyd! Yer mum'd whip ya black 'n' blue...*

"Maybe they wanna give us the experience. Serge did say he'd be within a click of us, right?"

"Fair dues. But if da rumours are gen, 'n' dese are terrorists, dey wouldn't be takin' chances, would dey? Dey wouldn't send two crows like us, ya get me?"

"The terrorist fing's been blown up out all proportion, I reckon. We're just 'ere to observe 'n' report, serge said. The attack was a couple of towns down the road." Gurdeep points to their left. "See? That smoke's some way from 'ere."

Floyd frowns as he follows his squadmate's finger: he espies another UAV. "So ya reckon it's just a rescue job?"

"I reckon we should just trust the Ruperts 'n' do as we're told. They didn't go to Sandhurst for nuffin, did they?"

"Which brings me onto da next ting I was gonna say."

"Which is?"

"I'm not sure I'm cut out for dis army business."

"Fucksake, fam. Bit late to say that now, innit? Don't worry, I'll look after yer ol' mum for ya."

"Not dat I'm scared o' dyin' or anyfin'. 'N' leave my mum out of it, ya prick."

Gurdeep jogs the final few yards to the emaciated treeline that separates nature from suburbia, while Floyd covers from a crouching position. After a moment and a few hand signals, the former returns the favour as the latter squelches across the soggy field. "So what is it, then?"

"What's what?" Private Nelson has eyes on the community centre they've been ordered to secure.

"Fuckin' 'ell, do you 'ave to make an effort to be this dense, or does it come naturally? What's the reason ya don't think this is for you?"

"Just… followin' orders when dey don't make no sense… it doesn't sit right wiv me, ya get me?"

"Maybe they'll make sense when we're done. Anyway, time to get down to business. Standard breach 'n' clear, innit. Probable civvy presence, so we go in cold as my ex's pussy."

Within thirty seconds, they've gained access to the hut, which is deserted. Foldaway chairs are arrayed in rows, and there are plastic cups and a half empty jug of cordial on a trestle table at the head of the room.

Floyd's wondering whether to update his commanding officer, when an exclamation from Gurdeep stalls him. "What's up?"

"Is that… blood?"

"Where?"

Singh points his SA80 at a dark patch on the beige linoleum beneath the refreshments table.

"Could be. Funny smell in 'ere too. I'll radio in now."

"'N' tell 'em what? You know what the CO said. Check out the community centre. Then clear the playground 'n' the nursery."

"But dat blood —"

"— Could be someone's nosebleed. We ain't 'eard no shots. We ain't seen shit worth reportin'. Let's do as we're told, 'n' maybe, *just maybe*, we won't get our arseholes chewed out by serge."

"K. Come on, den." Floyd's gaze lingers on the ebony/crimson stain as he follows his fellow serviceman out into the open. *Ain't no nosebleed. Too much claret for dat.*

They're circumnavigating the small building when an explosion to their west puts a flock of birds to the wing and Floyd's heart in his gullet. "Da fuck?" He slams back first into corrugated steel and holds his weapon to his chest.

Keeping low, Gurdeep scrambles towards the corner of the hut. He pauses for a heartbeat before risking a peek around the side of the building. "All clear," he hisses. "Smoke's in the distance. Lot of it, though."

Then comes the gunfire. Most of it is small arms, assault rifles at the most, but the deeper bass of heavy machine gun fire is also unmistakable. Above them, an aeroplane the size of a bomber trundles by; streams of fumes pour from its underside.

Joining his buddy, Floyd keeps watch on the column of black fumes on the horizon whilst scanning the street before them. There are two cars in the middle of the road. One has a crushed nose; the other is blackened by fire. Beside the first there's a pool of blood, in which glass splinters glint like rubies in the early sun. A couple of rats, lapping at the scarlet spill, scamper underneath the crashed vehicles.

"Definitely some shit goin' down 'round 'ere," says Floyd, his rifle ready. "We ain't evacuatin' or rescuin' nobody."

"Well, the community centre peeps musta gone somewhere." Leading the way, Gurdeep heads for the end of Guppy Avenue, where it intersects with a larger street. "They ain't just vanished, 'ave they?"

Floyd sniffs the air. The smell of burning is getting stronger, and there's a chemical undertone now. "Shit!"

"What?" Gurdeep is on the driveway of the only house on the street.

"Da inhalers."

"Oh yeah."

The two soldiers fish in their pockets for the devices they were prescribed barely four hours ago. Both take two hits each.

"Right," Gurdeep turns back towards the big detached building. A year-old Mercedes saloon is parked on the drive, next to a new-looking campervan. The home's windows are curtained; there's no sign of anyone getting ready for a day at the office. "Front door's open. Only slightly, but... bit weird, innit?"

He's right. Icy fingers creep up Floyd's spine; he half-smirks at his trepidation. *Probably just let da cat out, or sometin'. Nuttin' to worry about. We be big, bad soldiers.*

Slinging their weapons over shoulders, the squaddies approach the doorstep. Gurdeep makes a visible effort to relax before rapping on the black door. His knock pushes it wider. He grimaces, as does Floyd; the stench of corruption is evident.

Using the building clearance tactics drilled into them a few short months ago, the pair investigate the house. Their ground floor inspection is interrupted upon entry to the conservatory. Collapsed on a couch, next to an overturned glass table, lies a middle-aged man. Dozens of flies are disturbed as the soldiers confirm the fellow's death. The settee is of brown leather, which is encrusted with blood.

"Jesus," Floyd says as they realise how the resident died. His throat, collarbones and the top of his chest have been savaged to the bone.

"Like a fuckin' bear's been at 'im." Gurdeep opens the conservatory's external door and breathes deeply. "Saw this YouTube vid once —"

"— Don't wanna know, mate. 'Bout time we talked to control, eh?"

"Yeah. We better secure —"

A bump upstairs; both men are alert.

"Time to earn our glorious pay." This time Floyd takes the lead. His nerves are jangling, his pulse pounding in his ears. The prospect of meeting the same end as the man downstairs is chastening, but there's also an excitement. *Gonna prove myself. Gonna prove I* am *cut out for dis. Show Corporal Hulmes 'n' his wanker mates I's not to be fucked wiv.*

He has to make a conscious effort not to rush up the stairs. Behind him, Gurdeep seems less keen. Maybe he's trying to stay cool too. The first floor's doors are all shut. Chandeliers hang from the ceiling, but none are lit, so it's almost dark. Something moves in one of the rooms. Nelson and Singh freeze.

Nothing happens for a few seconds, and they continue. Each bedroom and both bathrooms are empty. They finish in the master bedroom, which is meticulously tidy. Gurdeep's giving Sergeant Haveringham a sit-rep via his headset when a fluttering of the room's blinds attracts Floyd's attention. The window's opens, so he investigates: a shed is directly below. A child is on the roof. "Hey, dere!" Floyd calls. "Hang on."

The girl, who's roughly eleven or twelve years of age, looks up. Her pale face is marred with dirt, her brown hair matted. Save for a split lip, she looks uninjured. She wears pyjamas, slippers and an expression of bewilderment.

"Who is it?" Gurdeep asks, moving past the king-sized bed.

"Report, Private." The sergeant's disembodied tone, in both privates' ears, is urgent. "Are they hostile? Over."

"No, Sergeant!" Floyd snaps. "Nelson here. They are not hostile. I repeat, not hostile. Over."

"Private Singh. Lieutenant Pirie here. Do you concur? Are they hostile? Over."

Gurdeep peers out of the window, as does Floyd. The kid is now on the neatly-trimmed lawn and is heading for the back fence. "Not hostile, sir. Over."

A conversation ensues at the other end of the line, but it's too low for the two servicemen to hear.

Then: "Fire," barks Pirie. "Eliminate the threat! Over."

Privates Nelson and Singh look each other in the eye for a few moments, both blinking and sweating. The former shakes his head; the latter shrugs.

Chapter 30 — Lena Adderley — 07:30

Can't breathe.

Can't breathe, can't breathe.

"Ye left me, Lena." Lunt shakes his bowling ball head in reproach. "Ah came tae rescue ye, 'n' ye left me. That wisnae very nice, was it?"

But I had to save myself, Harry. We would've both died had I waited for you. What's the point in that?

"Called bein' a human. No' a fuckin' sociopath like you."

I'm sorry, Harry. What more can I say than 'I'm sorry'? How many times do I have to apologise?

Can't breathe, can't move —

Her eyes flicker open. She *can* breathe, after all, but she cannot move.

Am I paralysed? Oh god, please don't let me be paralysed, with all those freaks running around. I'd rather be fucking dead.

She opens her mouth, and her mandibles still work. She turns her head from side to side, so her neck, though sore, remains functional. Although she can't see much – a cracked windscreen twelve inches from her face if she looks up, and a great, white mass everywhere else – at least she's not blind. The smell of fuel and blood is in her nostrils. A wind whistles nearby. And, it seems, her sense of touch is operational, though all she can feel is a yielding pressure, as if she's cocooned in a giant amniotic sac.

However, her legs are immobile. At first she panics, concluding she is permanently disabled, until she realises that she can in fact move them. Only very slightly, yet she has feeling and muscular control from her hips to her toes. There's no pain, but the bottom half of her body is trapped somehow. The object holding her shins and thighs in place isn't like the white bubble around her torso. It's hard and unforgiving, like the jaws of some giant crocodile.

Then she realises: the big white thing's an airbag. The van crashed as she was trying to escape Mortborough.

Serves me right for leaving Harry.

Lena can't recall the collision itself. Was it caused by the bombardment, or by human error? Her last recollection was hearing the first missile land, about a mile away, as she headed towards the motorway slip road. Actually, no... she was on the dual carriageway, about to pass under one of the motorway bridges... two demented zombies launched themselves over the railing...

Squeezing her eyes shut, she strives to remember more, unsuccessfully. Now, for the first time, she's starting to hurt. Not anywhere in particular – she's sure she's not broken any bones and doesn't believe she's actively bleeding – but every part of her body aches or stings. Her hands are scratched and shredded, her arm and back muscles strained, by climbing factory fences. The crash caused myriad injuries, as yet unidentified.

Plus, she's ravenously hungry and thirsty. Were she not, she could happily go back to sleep, surrender to oblivion. She's no longer driven to protect her family's legacy or prevent the destruction of her hometown. That ship has long sailed. The world she inhabited twenty-four hours ago no longer exists. If she ever escapes from the van-cum-prison, she will eat food and drink fluids, but after that, what will she do?

She could hand herself in to the police. Explain that she's partially culpable for the worst man-made disaster in human history. Be held accountable for her foolishness. Share Sofia Aslam's theories on a possible remedy for the zombie apocalypse. Except she would never see the inside of a courtroom, for Villeneuve or his allies would ensure some 'accident' befell her before she could ever implicate the Government.

Of course, any decision over her next course of action is moot. She can't move, let alone save the world or self-martyrise. Her legs are so tightly bound she's surprised they're not shattered. If she could move them even just an inch or two, she might be able to manoeuvre herself into a better position, but she can't. Her arms are relatively mobile, though with the airbag deployed, there's no room to move.

Shouldn't it have deflated by now? The crash was hours ago, at midnight or thereabouts. Judging by the light she can see in her peripheral vision, day has dawned. Lena's sure she read somewhere that airbags deflate after a while. The one half-smothering her must've malfunctioned. If, however, she can remove its bulk, she may be able to use her hands to free her lower body.

Hang on, a hairpin. That'd do it. Bursting the damned thing could be dangerous, but so could being stuck in this bloody van.

With difficulty, she gets her right hand up and over her head. It brushes against the rearview mirror in the process. Her scalp is sore, moist and sticky; she's cut herself. More importantly, her hair is loose. The pin is gone.

She lets out a low growl of frustration. *That fucking airbag is here to stay.*

Maybe someone will pass by, and she can summon help. With this in mind, she closes her eyes and breathes more shallowly. Somebody could walk past, so she needs to be alert.

*Some*thing *could come. A zombie rather than a person. And I'll be shouting away, asking to become some undead bastard's breakfast.*

Nevertheless, she listens. Over the next five minutes, she hears an explosion, two volleys of gunfire, something like a scream, the calls of birds, the rustle of a windborne piece of rubbish, the far away screech of tyres and, most commonly, the rumble of her own stomach. But no passers-by.

"There must be *something* I can do," Lena mutters. *Surely this isn't the end. Starved and dehydrated, packed into this van like a vacuum-sealed side of beef.*

Movement outside sets her heart a race. She almost yells and has to bite her own lip. *Could be anything out there.* Ambiguity taunts her; the footsteps are slightly irregular, but not blatantly those of the walking dead. No one is talking, though it sounds like there's only one pedestrian at large. She could err on the side of caution, presume the worst, remain silent and pray the stranger leaves her be. Or should she reveal herself and hope for the best? While the former could mean the chance of potential salvation is missed, the latter may lead to discovery by man-eating ghouls.

Shit, shit, shit. What to do?

Is it her imagination, or is the mysterious individual increasing their pace? Now it's within ten yards. And now no more than five.

Wincing, Lena fills her lungs. She mouths the word 'help' as if practicing. Ludicrously, she feels self-conscious, almost embarrassed by her dilemma.

A snarl outside strangles the cry in her throat. *Shit. One of them. Please keep going. Please fuck off and leave me alone.*

The footfalls are slowing, becoming more measured.

Please leave me alone. Her top lip trembles; sweat pricks her flesh.

Another vocalisation.

It's going to smash the windows, drag me out and fucking eat me. I'm going to die painfully, so painfully. This is karma, my punishment for leaving Harry. A squirt of urine escapes Lena's bladder, trickling into knickers already damp with perspiration.

The third utterance is quieter, as though the 'speaker' has turned away. Shambling footsteps recommence as the creature loses interest and departs.

Lena breathes a long deep breath. She follows with several more, making a conscious effort to calm herself.

Shit. The inhaler. I'll be clawing my way out of here as one of them *if I don't keep up my dose.*

She can't reach her pocket, however, not with the airbag and crumpled parts of van holding her in place.

So that's it. This will be her end: transformed into a mindless cannibal by the very chemical she greenlit. She will die, and she will be resurrected, like the crops Evolve were targetting, like the people of Mortborough and elsewhere since yesterday. If and when the general public learn of her death, they will say she deserved it. Her actions have caused so much suffering; now it's her turn.

I didn't know this would happen, though!

"No, you didn't, Lena," she whispers. "But you put success over safety. You ignored the expert, and this is the result."

Even if she didn't deliberately cause the apocalypse, that isn't her only crime. She knowingly left Lunt to perish in order to save her own skin and her family's reputation.

But he had a death wish! There was no way he'd escape Evolve HQ alive. Staying with him would've been suicide.

To a degree, she can absolve herself of Harry's demise. His determination to throw away his life for an unachievable goal was as ludicrous as Lena risking death to save the Adderley name. All that matters now is survival, she decides. Everything else is merely detail.

There will be a way of extricating herself from this tomb; she simply hasn't yet worked it out. First things first. She needs to destroy this airbag, and then she can reassess. Opening her mouth, Lena tries to bite the bag, but she can't get any purchase. "Fuck!"

What else can I do?

The rearview mirror.

Pushing harder into the plastic cushion, she reaches up for the mirror. It's more difficult to remove than she would've guessed, though. Her restricted range of movement doesn't help, and before long, her shoulder is cramping. Nevertheless, Lena continues to work away. Back and forth she pulls; right and left she wrenches.

The fixing loosens quickly, but it reaches a point beyond which no further progress seems possible. She varies her approach; her wrist hurts more.

It's not going to work. I'm going to be stuck in here, until I eventually die and come back undead, or I starve to death, or another one of those freaks comes and gets me.

"Don't you fucking dare quit," she tells herself.

She imagines Naomi, her younger sister by one year, watching. Currently running her own cosmetics business in the States, she was something of a tom-boy as a child. She wasn't as academic as her older sister, but she was more physical. As tough as any of the boys at school, in fact. Although Naomi always looked out for her sibling when they were young, protecting her from bullies jealous of their family's fortune, she was never indulgent of weakness. She wanted Lena to stand up for herself.

"Ow!"

The mirror's surface has broken, grazing her hand. However, if she can prise a sliver of glass from its housing, she can use it to burst the airbag. She traces the outline of the spider-web crack, grimacing as a jagged edge slits her fingertip. Before long, she's found the centre of the web. Using her fingernail, she scrapes at the centre of the fracture. Fresh cuts open where nail meets flesh. Tears roll from her eyes. Blood tickles her hand, wrist and forearm.

A piece of glass comes free. And slips from her blood-slicked fingers. Lena almost roars in dismay, then in triumph as she feels a prick in her neck. The makeshift pin is within her grasp.

Now that there's no scratching-against-a-rearview-mirror noise, however, she hears a different sound. One not dissimilar from that she's been making herself. On the other side of the van, closer to her legs, something is worrying at metal. There's something else, too, something more organic. A slobbery, wet, urgent noise.

Oh, shit. Some kind of animal, perhaps… a zombie animal. Aslam said that might be possible.

She now grips the shard of mirror between forefinger and thumb. It'll slice the airbag open like a knife through butter and allow her to try and free her legs, but if the thing trying to get into the van actually sees her, it may redouble its efforts. Or it might not matter. The dog, or badger, or fox is probably using its sense of smell.

So what should she do?

Chapter 31 — Luke Norman — 08:25

"Why couldn't they just, like, *stay rescued?*"

"I dunno, Luke." Jada gives her best consolatory smile. "Just remember, they might be kids, but they have minds of their own. Things they wanna do."

Luke fiddles with the adjustment lever beneath his swivel chair. "Well, they picked the worst possible time t' rebel."

"We'll find 'em. Won't we, Josh?"

Gould gives a single nod. Sat at the computer in the mall's security office, he's in his element. Like everyone else in the cramped room, he's sweating, but he seems oblivious.

"'Ow long will it take?" asks Brad. "I'm 'ungry."

"Me too." Ashara sighs. "'N' I can't stand confined spaces. Wanna go grab a snack?"

"Yeah. Anybody else want anythin'?"

"I'm good, thanks," Jada replies.

Luke shakes his head irritably. He continues to stare at the monitor, but Gould's wizardry means nothing to him. Although Brad helped at first, his fellow IT expert became annoyed by his input. "You'll be able to access *all* of the shops' feeds, right?"

Gould's eyeroll is almost audible. "For the second time, yes. There's no reason why not. Now, if you'll just be quiet…"

When Luke bristles, Jada puts a hand on his knee. She's an attractive woman, as strong-willed and intelligent as she is pretty and sweet-natured. Under different circumstances, he would relish her attention, but at the moment, all he can think of is his failure. He did the hard part. Rescued his son while all hell was breaking loose in Mortborough, just in time to avoid the missile strike. They beat the odds.

Then I fucked up. Took my eye off the ball. 'N' Connor slipped through m' fingers. Kid's mum was right. I am *a waste o' space.*

It's not Luke's fault, Jada and Brad insist. Sometimes, shit happens. He should be glad his boy's still alive.

Maybe he's not alive, though. Maybe Connor and Evie were snapped up as soon as they left the Crawford Centre, pulled off their stolen bikes… His nostrils flare; his jaw clenches.

"They'll be okay." Jada pats his thigh.

"I know. I mean, I *don't* know, but thanks anyway."

"No need to thank me."

He puffs his cheeks. "I just… I wish I knew *why* he's gone. We've not seen much of each other, me 'n' Connor, so maybe he don't feel comfortable 'round me."

"Don't be daft. It's their mums. Just young kids who want their mums. That's all there is to it."

"So it's my fault, innit? I argued with 'em, wouldn't entertain the idea of goin' back t' Mortborough —"

"It's nobody's fault. You were doin' your best to keep them safe."

"I guess so. Sorry, I must be doin' yer 'ead in, goin' on 'n' on about it. Brad too, he's lost *everythin'*, 'n' I keep remindin' 'im all the time."

"Don't apologise. There's no manual for this. No one knows how to deal with shit like this. All we can do —"

"— Fuck!" Gould pushes the mouse away and slams the desk. "Fucking stupid bastard thing."

"What's the problem?" Luke snaps.

"You wouldn't understand."

"Would Brad?" Jada asks.

Gould snorts. "No. Well, maybe."

Luke stands, sending his seat spinning away. He catches his thigh on another desk as he exits the security room in a hurry. Out in the open mall, the lights are brighter. Blinking, he waves at Brad and Ashara, who, arms laden with junk food, are on their way back from their errand.

The pair don't rush. Luke becomes vexed but tries not to scowl at the pair. *They're tired. Everyone's tired. 'N' Connor gettin' away is* my *fuck-up, not theirs.*

Five minutes later, he has reason to smile. Brad filled Gould's knowledge gap, and, after a little bickering, the pair managed to hack into the Crawford Centre's CCTV suite. The latter now believes he can use the Crawford's system as a "stepping stone" to access other nearby surveillance programmes.

"'Ow is that even possible?" Ashara asks. "That's some mad shit."

"No point askin' him," Jada warns. "He won't tell you."

Tapping away at the keyboard, Gould wears his customary conceited expression. "I won't tell her, because she wouldn't understand. Only superior intellects like me, and to a much lesser extent Brad, would get it."

"Yes, mate, yer a genius." Luke, still standing, takes a bite from a chocolate bar. "But before ya start playin' 'round, can ya try 'n' find Connor 'n' Evie? Please?"

Under the assumption that the kids would've left the Centre by the exit closest to the bike shop, Gould accesses camera recordings. The chronological window is small, so they swiftly find footage of the children leaving the building.

Luke feels a queasy mixture of excitement and dread as he watches his son. "They're headin' west."

Brad's set his food aside and now looks downcast. "Towards Mortborough."

We can catch 'em. But we gotta move fast. "'Ow long before ya can get access to other cameras in the area, Gould?"

The bus station manager clicks his tongue. "Not long. I still have remote access to a programme I used at work. I can already pick up feeds in Mortborough, so now I'll add these Walkley cameras, too."

"So it's just the road from Walkley to Mortborough you need to add?" Jada says.

"It is."

The conversation becomes muted, as if Luke's underwater. He's still staring at the CCTV footage. Half a minute's passed since Connor and Evie cycled into view, but the stream's been playing in slow motion. Therefore, the zombies plodding across the screen were actually moving much quicker in real life. They were only a few seconds behind the kids. *Those fuckers could already be eatin' my boy...* "We 'ave to 'urry." He points at the video then starts to move towards the door.

"Hang on," says Jada, "we need to plan this out. Otherwise we'll never find them."

Ashara raises her hand, like she's at school. "Josh could stay 'ere, watch the CCTV 'n', like, guide us."

Brad frowns. "'Ow'll he 'guide' us, exactly? Our mobiles 'ave no signal, remember."

"Are there no, like, security guard bodies about?"

Brad and Jada have seen the most corpses and undead; they nod.

"So they'll probably 'ave walkie-talkies, won't they?"

Luke's already leaving. "Good thinking, Ashara."

Everyone but Gould and Ashara head to the department store. The exit Brad and Jada blocked is unbreached, though some of the windows are smashed. They find the first security officer within a minute; Luke pilfers his radio and a baton. A second is nowhere to be seen, however.

Luke stops at the top of an escalator. His vision is tinged red, his ears ringing. *We're gonna be too late. We're gonna be too late, 'n' Connor'll be caught, 'n' he'll be dead. 'N' it'll all be your fault.* "Ya sure there were two of 'em?"

"I think so." Brad glances at Jada, who looks pained.

"Fucksake!" Luke, now pacing, overturns a clothes rail in rage. "I'm gonna go after 'em. Fuck the walkie-talkies —"

"Woah!" says Jada. "Just *calm down*. Remember what we said yesterday, in the street, when that freak came outta the bushes?"

"What?" Luke's barely registering her words.

"We stick together. Whatever happens."

"Maybe we should check outside," says Brad. "If we see one through the window, we pull down the barricade, kill it, nick its radio."

Luke would rather do something than nothing. He draws the Glock, switches off the safety and goes back upstairs. Jada and Brad are close behind, checking their weapons as they walk. Together they remove the obstacles from the doorway. Sure enough, one of the monsters lurking outside wears a Crawford Centre uniform. The other two seem nervous of the zombies that begin to renew their assault on the doors, but Luke is heedless. Panic lends a speed and strength that can only last so long.

When they try to pull the final display cabinet away from the doors, a heavily-tattooed, leather-clad zombie reaching through the smashed window mindlessly grabs the fixture. They continue to pull; it holds on. The flesh on its arms snags and tears on jagged shards of glass in the window-frame. Its expression remains blank, its sole remaining eye almost entranced.

Using the nightstick, Luke bludgeons its fingers. Bone crunches; the creature releases its grip. Brad gathers himself then barrels into one of the double doors, knocking a slack-jawed adolescent girl to the ground. Immediately, he's up, swinging his axe as undead converge on their position. Bits of skin and streams of blood fly left and right.

Jada's to his right, firing her submachine gun. They're on a concourse. Ten yards away are escalators that lead down to a car park; beyond that is an archway, then an open air parking lot bathed in the morning sun. Luke batters a stocky former construction worker with his baton. Uses his Glock to chestshot and headshot an old woman zombie. Again he swings his cosh, tearing a formally-attired zomb's teeth from its gums. As he cracks open its skull, he feels bony, eager fingers at the nape of his neck. The MP5 spits; the grip weakens.

"There!" yells Jada.

The security guard, its left trouser leg torn to reveal a grisly mess of thigh muscle and exposed kneecap, is hobbling their way. Twice Jada's SMG fires, holing the mall cop's right shoulder and cheekbone. Like a chainsawn oak it falls. Luke spots a walkie-talkie attached to its belt.

Brad's occupied. His axe is lodged in the ribcage of a hair-netted fast-food cashier, so he's switching to his shotgun, but he doesn't have time to aim and has to use the gun as club.

While Jada offers covering fire, Luke hurdles bodies and crawling zombies. He slips on blood and goes down hard on one hand, sending lightning bolts of pain to his elbow. Cursing, he straightens up. Most of the undead have fallen, though there are more crossing the outdoor car park.

Where's the fuckin' security guy? Shit, there.

Looming over the prostrate guard, there's a woman wearing a baby-sling. Her mouth is a red ruin, stark against her porcelain forehead. A small head protrudes from the papoose, its hair matted and dark. *Hang on... is that kid... alive? Oh fuck... I can't kill a baby.*

The mother lurches forwards, filthy hands cutting the air.

Maybe I can take out the mum without gettin' the kid...

Suddenly, parent and child are upon Luke. The infant twists in its carrier, gums gnashing, as the adult lunges.

A double shotgun blast stops the unholy duo in its tracks, showering Luke with warm blood. The nightstick is wrenched from his grasp.

Luke blinks and gapes for a moment.

"Luke!" Jada shouts. "The radio!"

He nods and retrieves the device, then follows his comrades back into the Centre.

Seven minutes later, having re-blocked the department store entryway, they're with Gould and Ashara again. The former's keeping track of Connor and Evie, who are on Manchester Road, approximately halfway between Walkley and Mortborough. The latter – briefly an event steward at Manchester Arena – is giving a crash course on two-way radio operation. She'll stay with Josh, in case he needs to take a break.

"You good with that?" Jada asks as she, Luke and Brad prepare to leave.

"Damn right I am! I just wanna stay alive, get outta 'ere in one piece. Not that I don't wanna 'elp, like, just, ya know…

"You don't need to explain," Jada assures the younger woman. "Luke needs to get his boy. Brad's Luke's mate. I'm a nutter who'd risk her life to make a point. Most people aren't like us."

Despite the churning in his gut, Luke half-smiles. With considerable effort he stops watching his cycling son. "We ready?"

"Ready." Brad nods grimly.

Jada's demeanour is equally stern. "Let's go."

"On your way back," says Gould, "you might want to use the canal, if possible. I've noticed the zombies steer clear of water when they can. Plus, it runs within two hundred yards of here."

Ashara and Gould wish them luck, even though they'll be maintaining frequent contact by radio. They exit the mall using the same toilet window through which they entered. From there, blinking against the strengthening sun, they head to the closest residential street, where they find the abandoned milk float Ashara noticed on the CCTV feed.

Their luck is good for once, for the electric vehicle's in working order. Once they've removed the crates of spoiling milk, they're on their way, with Jada at the wheel. The queasiness in Luke's stomach lessens. The float's engine is relatively quiet; on the way to the A road the children are using, three streets in all, they pass two zombie mobs. Neither group notices the humans till they've passed.

"Ya hear that?" Brad asks when they've been on Manchester Road for a minute.

Luke frowns. "All I can hear is this thing's motor, 'n' those fuckin' planes that keep flyin' over."

Jada shrugs. "What's the deal with that plane, anyway? Looks like it's trailin' smoke."

"Nah. It's not the plane I can 'ear. It's somethin' else. Somethin' closer." Hanging onto the rear right-hand side's roof support, Brad swings out to look above them. "Shit. We got a fan."

"What?" Luke copies his friend, leaning to the float's left. "It's a drone. Not necessarily a bad thing —"

"— You takin' the piss? D'ya know 'ow much money the UK Government's spent on weaponised drones the last coupla years?"

"Let's 'ope it's not weaponised, then. Jada, can't this piece o' shit go any faster —"

It only takes one burst of deafening drone cannon fire to immobilise the milk cart.

"Run!" Luke yells.

Chapter 32 — Lena Adderley — 9:10

She's never been one for eternal optimism, but somehow, the Evolve chief executive has half-convinced herself that the animal continuing to besiege the special forces van might be benign in nature.

Perhaps it's just her brain's way of making her last breaths easy. After all, being mauled by some hell hound would be painful enough. So why endure mental torture first? Ignorance is bliss. Let death take her unawares, if it must come. The nice doggy might be trying to help her. Like the Rough Collie in that old TV show.

Bullshit. It'll get in eventually, and when it does, you'd better hope it goes for your throat. 'Cause some dogs go for the face. Get a grip, Lena, and start thinking of a way out of this mess.

Maybe, when the inquisitive creature's found a way in, she can use its point of entry as a way out, once she's negated the canine threat. She still has the sliver of rearview mirror glass. If she can quickly poke the beast in both eyes as soon as it gets in, she could take it by surprise. Then she'll cut its throat.

You won't see it, though, you idiot. It'll just appear from behind the airbag, and you won't know it's there till it's munching away.

In fact, the dog will probably burst the airbag with its claws and teeth. Which might scare it, or, at least, distract it. *If that's the case, then, why not just pop the airbag yourself?* "Good point, Lena," she mutters.

She holds the glass blade aloft, ready to plunge it into the plastic. *Hang on. Should I do it now, so I can be ready, or when the animal is in, so I can shock it?* Instinctively, she favours the first option. For a start, it'll rid her of the burdensome balloon. Plus she'll be able to assume a better defensive position.

And shit, how did I forget?

The gun she stole yesterday from a paramilitary is somewhere in the cabin. Whether it has any ammunition left is a different matter, but even if she has to use it as a blunt force weapon, it'll prove more effective than a small shard of glass.

The creature's getting closer. In fact, the noise it's making is different, as though it's tearing at something new. Which means it's progressing. If Lena shuts her eyes and breathes shallowly, she fancies she can hear it panting. A low growl in its throat. Being zombified turns humans far more aggressive, so perhaps it does likewise with animals. Dogs can be extremely vicious without any help. An undead one could be as deadly as a wolf.

Definitely getting closer. It'll be sinking its teeth in soon, ripping away my flesh, gorging on my muscle and organs, chewing on my bones...

Her hands are shaking now. She's sweating profusely, breathing quicker. Bowels and bladder contracting, eyes and nose streaming.

I need to get out!

Licking salty tears and perspiration from her top lip, Lena fingers the edge of the mirror splinter. It's sharp. But so are the dog's teeth.

A crunching sound from the dog's direction.

She plunges the glass into the airbag, and for the briefest moment, nothing happens. Then the giant bubble collapses in on itself. Her stomach lurches as her torso drops, but she falls no more than six inches before hitting the driver side car seat. She's still covered by plastic, though it's soft and yielding now, in large flaps.

Lena realises how her legs are trapped: the lower half of the front left of the vehicle is crumpled into a low-slung sports car. Somehow, the windscreen and both side windows are intact. Lena presumes the van must've mounted the kerb at speed and gained some air before it hit the parked car. The left-hand side of the dashboard is protruding into the cabin space, holding her lower body fast.

The machine gun is in the footwell by the accelerator and brake pedals, partially covered by the deflated airbag. A white and grey husky is at the window – which is open an inch – scrabbling and gnawing at the crack. A pink froth of blood and saliva stains the glass. Suddenly, the canine sees its prey for the first time. Cold eyes widen as the big beast attacks with renewed vigour. It manages to get a ragged paw through the gap.

Slowly, Lena reaches out for the gun. She doesn't want to alarm the big beast, for it might become even more frantic. Once she's shot it, she can focus on freeing her legs.

Then something flashes in the corner of her eye. Both the dead dog and Lena look down the road. While the former quickly loses interest in the trio of zombies lumbering their way, the latter does not. *Shit. They'll smash straight in.*

The four-legged freak will have to wait; the bipeds are now her priority. Two were once women in their thirties, the third a young boy. The females move slowly, seemingly unfocussed, but the youngster is in a hurry. Within seconds it's up on the bonnet, headbutting the windscreen.

Grimacing, the trapped woman grabs the gun, raises the barrel and closes her eyes as she blows the little zomb away. Shattered glass showers Lena; her ears ring. Now the windscreen's gone. The child's slid away. Dumbly, the dog's still trying to get in via the passenger-side door. Sweeping glass from her face, Lena aims at the pair of zombies still heading her way. They're within ten yards.

It's an easy shot. But when she squeezes the trigger, nothing happens.

Oh, no. Out of ammo.

One of the monsters is faster than its sister, but when it reaches the van it trips. There's a solid clunk as its head strikes the vehicle's bumper. Zombess number two stumbles over number one and lands heavily, face first, on the van's hood. Then the second disappears from view, presumably grabbed by the first as it hauls itself upright. Lena would laugh at the stapstick sequence if she wasn't about to die.

And now both of the demons are standing. They're climbing onto the —

Bang bang bang bang bang bang bang.

What the fuck was that?

Whatever it was, it's shot the pair of predators to pieces. A fine red mist lands on Lena's face, so she cuffs it away, disgusted. The zombie bodies are riddled with large calibre bullet holes. A whirring sound jerks Lena's attention skyward. A black drone hovers above the road, twenty feet off the ground, about fifteen yards from the van. After a moment, it flies overhead then away.

Dog.

It's been distracted by the drone and zombies. As Lena desperately tries to squirm free, the animal lopes around the front of the van, stopping to sniff at the three fallen undead.

Now that she can see what she's doing, Lena reckons she'll be able to extricate her legs from the mangled steel. But will she manage it time? She bites back a sob as something hard and sharp scores her left calf. She whimpers as her right knee jars against a blunt protrusion. Her left leg is all but loose, the ragged trousers visible as far as her ankle. If she can just twist her ankle —

Claws scrape metal as the husky leaps onto the bonnet. It sees Lena and bares murderous teeth. She points her gun, a useless gesture. Then one of the dog's ears twitches. It looks over its shoulder for a moment.

Her left leg is out.

What's that noise? Is it… a bicycle? No, two. And they're going past me, back into Mortborough. Who the hell's going back there?

The hound jumps off the van and darts away.

With her left leg extracted, Lena has space to pull her right clear too. She does so and sits up straight, just in time to see two cycling children, a straw-haired girl – who looks strangely familiar – and a darker boy, turn off the main road. The zombie mutt's in pursuit, but its gait is awkward. Hopefully, it's injured and won't be able to catch the cyclists.

Why's it gone after them when I was a sitting duck? Perhaps its instinct to chase overrode its hunger. But do the living dead even have the same instincts anymore?

Gingerly, she climbs out of the vehicle. The entire bottom half of her body, from navel to toes, is in fresh pain, but it doesn't feel as if she's incurred any permanent damage. Her upper body is still sore from climbing industrial unit fences the previous day.

For the first time since the airbag burst, she appraises her surroundings. Turton Road is on the very edge of town. A hundred yards away, it forks, with one direction leading to the motorway, the other the A-road to Walkley. There are no houses nearby, just a public house, a couple of shops, a bus stop and a modern-looking office building. All she can smell is dust and burning. Save for an occasional rattle of gunfire or minor explosion, silence reigns. The sun is bright, the skies blue; a huge aeroplane is dumping some kind of gas.

Some sort of antidote? The same chemical in the inhalers, maybe, being distributed to neighbouring towns, just as Sofia Aslam recommended.

Lena needs to find another means of transport. There's a large auto dealership nearby; perhaps she can steal a car.

What about the kids, though? They're riding right into undead central.

They're not her responsibility. Her father needs her at home – if the family seat in Cheshire hasn't already been ransacked. She pictures the scene for a moment, the stately halls puddled with blood. Nurses and domestic servants murdered and half-eaten, or stumbling around, undead, looking for meat. Her old daddy won't have been affected by airborne Resurrex, because Lena sent inhalers for him and all his staff. But medicated or not, they won't be immune if bitten.

She takes a triple hit on her inhaler, which is somehow still intact. She starts walking towards the car showroom. Limping at first, but the stiffness and pain begin to recede. As she turns onto Salford Lane, a narrow residential street lined with wasting trees, she disturbs a murder of crows. The birds were gathered around a small body; Lena quickly averts her gaze.

Slowly, she comes to a stop. The vehicle sales centre is about eighty yards away, the 'Hesketh Norton' sign now visible. However, the way is blocked. There are undead in the road, so she turns on her heel and heads back the way she's come.

She's soon passing the battered black van, the red coupe underneath and the three slain zombies. Every step takes her closer to death, past houses increasingly stricken by missiles. She needs to find another way out of town. *Maybe the kids I saw earlier know a better route?*

A few minutes ago, the children turned off Turton and onto Brazier Avenue, so Lena does the same. There are houses with gardens on Brazier, which means more places to hide for friends and foes. She scans the yards for the bicycles – one blue, the other purple – and the zombie dog.

What catches her eye, however, is something entirely unexpected. At the next crossroads, a group of black-clad soldiers scurry into view. They hunker down behind a burnt-out SUV, with a couple aiming over the bonnet. Their rifle stocks twitch; whiplash reports follow an instant later.

Then one looks to his left. He points. The guns swing to bear on Lena.

Chapter 33 — Floyd Nelson — 9:40

The pyjama-wearing girl's scream replays in his head every minute or so. He can see her face, aghast with fear, when he blinks. Blood squirting from the bullet wound in her throat, painting the fence that was just too high for her climb.

He's always been cursed with an over-active imagination. His mother vacillates between chiding him for 'having his head in the clouds', and boasting that his creative gift is god-given. In any case, he and Gurdeep disobeyed a direct order. They did not shoot the fleeing child; they could not shoot the fleeing child. Even if King Charles III himself had demanded the youngster's death, Floyd wouldn't have pulled the trigger.

Another large aeroplane thunders through the heavens above. The Government are obviously dropping chemicals of some sort, and they've been doing so all morning.

"'Ow close did ya come?" Gurdeep asks for the second time. "To, ya know, smokin' —"

"I know what ya mean." Floyd checks over the hedge one more time, before moving off the lawn and over the road. He stops and crouches behind a bus shelter, covering his mate as he crosses the street. "Touch 'n' go, bruv. Trigger finger twitchin'," he lies.

"I'll be honest. I came pretty close. Direct order, 'n' everyfin'. Gurdeep uses exactly the same words as he did earlier, when they were hiding from a drone in a drive-through coffee shop.

"I feel ya." *Not in a million years, bruv. Rather shoot myself dan some random yout.*

Sticking to one's principals has consequences, however.

"That church, right?"

"Right. Somewhere to think. Decide what to do next." *Maybe God'll tell us.*

They scan the next street and see no danger. Keeping low, they dash over another road, using abandoned cars as waypoints. Thirty seconds later, they're crossing Saint Stephen's churchyard and pushing the oaken doors wide. It's dark inside. And quiet. There's an outdoors smell, damp timber, as if they're in the woods rather than a place of worship.

After a swift inspection, Gurdeep sits on a pew but keeps his rifle trained on the entrance. "Mad shit, bruv."

"Watch yer language," Floyd replies in a whisper.

"Sorry, my bad. Forgot ya were religious."

"I ain't. Not really. Just… ya know, bitta respect."

"Still can't believe they wanted us to shoot that kid."

"I know. It's on top."

"So what's the sitch, then?"

Floyd sighs and rubs his eyes with the heel of his hand. "Dunno. Sometin' don't feel right. Dey been talkin' 'bout terrorists, but I reckon we gettin' played."

Gurdeep stands and walks halfway down the aisle, his gaze intent on the altar. His footsteps are surreally-loud, his posture tense. "Whaddya mean? Played by who?"

"Maybe *we're* the terrorists."

"Yer makin' no sense."

"Dem orders made no sense. What I'm sayin' is maybe da terrorists 'ave infiltrated da brass."

"Nah."

"'Ow d'ya explain it, den?"

"There'll be some explanation." On his way back now, Gurdeep is staring into the gloomy rafters.

Unlike his squadmate, Floyd ignores the flutter of pigeon wings above. "Sometin's wrong, Gurd. I can feel it, like an instinct, ya know?"

"Terrorists use kids. Not remember trainin'? Story 'bout that corporal in Afghan? Eight year-old wiv a bomb-vest, bruv."

"Yeah. But dat was Afghan. This is da UK, innit. Dat kid wasn't no terrorist."

"But that's 'ow they get ya. Mind games, innit. They're smart, them terrorists."

"Yer wrong, Gurd. Dat girl was terrified."

"Yeah, okay, she did look pretty scared. All I'm sayin' is I trust the Army. They know best. If they said to kill 'er, there'll be a reason."

"Can't see no good reason for slottin' a ten year-old, bruv."

They to-and-fro for a while. Eventually, they agree to disagree, accepting that formulating a plan is the priority. The facts are thus: they disregarded orders; their comms have been remotely-disabled; drones have opened fire on them twice; and they've been separated from their unit for nearly three hours.

They've speculated about the above when they've not been arguing over the significance and validity of the directive to kill pyjama-girl.

Floyd contends that their headsets were deliberately rendered inoperative, because they're no longer trusted. Gurdeep blames equipment malfunction. Whatever the reason, they are now incommunicado.

While Gurdeep reckons the UAVs attacked in error, Floyd believes they're now marked men. Either way, the fact remains: the gun-drones are a threat which needs to be avoided.

Alienation from the rest of the taskforce is similarly-debated. Floyd's happy to steer clear, because he thinks they'll be shot on sight; Floyd isn't so sure. The latter does accept, however, that they should keep a low profile. Lieutenant Pirie and the boys could welcome them back to the fold with open arms. But it's not worth the risk. So they decide to keep moving. They'll continue west, towards Mortborough, away from Manchester and the rest of their company, until they come up with a better idea.

The two privates emerge from St Stephen's, squinting against the sunlight. Mundane sounds, like birdsong and wind in the desiccated graveyard trees, are amplified. Hoping for fresh air, Floyd is disappointed. The reek of burning plastic is pervasive.

"Hear that?" Gurdeep asks as they make their way around the church.

"Armour?" Floyd looks both ways at a junction.

"Yeah. Thought we were the only team in town."

"Reckon we'll be proved wrong 'bout a lotta tings before dis is over."

A right turn leads to a broader thoroughfare, which features the usual working class haunts. Bookmakers, a pub, pawn shops, beauty salons, a taxi rank. Swinford Road, long and straight, also provides an eastward view ranging over two hundred yards.

"'N' dere's the armour." Floyd ducks behind a fire-ravaged hatchback.

"Challenger 3 main battle tank," Gurdeep says reverently. "Always wanted to be in the 'Chavalry', ya know."

"Well, if ya keep standin' dere like dat, ya might get da honour o' bein' run over by dem."

The pawnshop's door is ajar, so the two soldiers run inside.

"Can't believe they left it unlocked. All this gear. Jewellery. Probably loadsa cash, too, in the back."

"Evac, innit. No time to waste." *Sometin's not right about dis.*

A couple of minutes crawl by. The tanks treads and engine get louder, and soon, there's the sound of boots on the ground. Once they're sure the detachment has gone past, Floyd and Gurdeep exit the shop. One of the broken down cars has been shunted aside by the Challenger; shattered glass reflects sun rays getting stronger by the hour.

Using sidestreets running parallel with Bolton Road, they hurry to overtake the column. They don't want to get caught between units. Nor do they fancy being detected by drones. Therefore, they travel with as much stealth as possible, sprinting from corner to corner, using car shells and dying hedgerows as cover. Fifteen minutes later, they're in the clear. They've also circumnavigated Swinford town centre in the process.

Twice they spotted lone civilians – one man dressed scruffily, like a homeless person, and a woman in her twenties, stumbling around in confusion – but on both occasions they gave the people a wide berth.

Next, they take a shortcut through an industrial estate. There's more UAV activity overhead, so they've slowed their pace.

"Still fink we shoulda spoken to them civvies." Gurdeep is on his haunches, his back to a telephone exchange box.

Floyd shakes his head. "Nah, fam." He studies the sky with eyes slitted against the sun. "Sometin' funny about dem. I'm tellin' ya —"

"Aw, fuck off wiv all that voodoo shit, Floyd. You don't know shit I don't."

"Ain't voodoo, bruv. Why you gotta make dis about race? Just cause I got roots in da Caribbean, don't mean I's chupid."

"Ain't about race. 'Bout you bein' a dumb fuck. 'Ow can ya tell somefin' was wrong wiv 'em from forty yards away?"

"Dunno. Just... dey was actin' strange. Ya can't deny dat, Gurd. Dey didn't look like ordinary peeps mindin' dey own business, ya get me?"

"Yeah, alright. They looked weird. Maybe they was in shock, or somefin'. Ya know, mentally ill, then all this evac shit started, 'n' they just flipped out, like."

"Maybe. But sometin' don't —"

"— Feel right." Gurdeep huffs. "Yeah, I know, ya said —"

"— Be honest wiv me, fam. Does *nuttin* seem unusual 'bout all dis? Bein' ordered to kill kids. Tanks on da street. Planes droppin' chemicals 'n' shit all over. Peeps wanderin' about like dey in a trance or sometin'. It's fubar, bruv." Something in his peripheral vision. "Drone! Get down!"

A volley of cannon fire riddles the factory closest to the telephone exchange. Glass shatters, and something explodes inside the factory.

They flee. They take cover behind an abandoned lorry, until they realise the vehicle's contents could be flammable.

"In there!" Gurdeep yells, pointing at a warehouse, which has an open roller shutter entrance.

Dodging discarded pallets and plant machinery, the squaddies cross the distribution depot's front yard. High-calibre slugs whistle past them, chipping concrete, shattering windows, spreading dust. Both men drop to their bellies and roll under the shutter door.

"Fuckin' 'ell!" The armour-piercing rounds have left multiple holes in the steel rollers, so Gurdeep moves to one side of the entryway.

As does Floyd, on the opposite side. "Ya still fink dey attackin' us 'in error', Gurd?"

"Okay, okay. This is fucked up, bruv."

"Cluster. Fuck."

The storehouse is small, its floor space half an acre at the most. Judging by the haphazardly-positioned forklift trucks and pallets, it appears to have been deserted mid-shift. The lights are off, though. There's an unwholesome smell in the air, as though food has been left to turn rancid.

"Gonna see if it's still out there." The Sikh drops to a squat and peers out of the warehouse. "The drone."

"Be careful, fam."

"It is still there. Bit further away. Don't look like it's focussed on us, though. Keeps zippin' about, proper fast."

"Reckon I could take it?" Private Floyd Nelson was top of his class in marksmanship training.

"Yeah. If yer quick."

Floyd mimics his friend, then turns onto his front and looks down the iron sights of his SA80. The UAV – squat, black, almost featureless – is facing to the north. Its gun fires for a second, pauses, and fires again. Then it swoops and veers to its right, before ascending again. Even from at least a hundred yards' distance, the cannon is loud. *Dat's some firepower it's got.* "D'ya fink it's da same one dat's been followin' us?"

"Maybe." Gurdeep stands and begins a slow circuit of the warehouse. "Hard to say. All look the same to me.

Now he uses the ACOG sight to aim, tracking the machine as it scoots back and forth. "Ya fink I got enough firepower?"

"Dunno. Only one way to find out."

"Dey shoulda give me a Sharpshooter. 7.62mm NATO. Or a Barrett 50 cal."

"Well, you ain't a Septic, so you'll never get a Barrett. Just shoot the fuckin' bastard."

So he does. Three rounds hit the drone, dead centre, and it goes down without ceremony.

"Ya get it?"

"Damn right."

"Fuckin' yes, bruv! 'Ang on… ain't that, like, treason or somefin'?"

"Maybe. Kill or be killed, bruv."

Gurdeep begins to pace. "Fuck. We'll be court-marshalled. No doubt."

"Shoulda thought o' dat *before* I smoked it," Floyd says, affecting insouciance. *He's right. We outlaws now.* "Anyway, it's just a piece o' metal. Dey can repair it. Come on. Let's go." He rolls under the shutters and out of the depot.

His squadmate follows suit, and they both scour the skies for a moment, seeing nothing but birds and wispy clouds.

Floyd frowns at something close to the horizon. He uses his rifle scope to get a better view. "UAV spotted. But it's miles away."

"Where? I can't…" Gurdeep falls silent. "What the fuck?"

A person is emerging from behind the HGV the guardsmen used as cover five minutes ago. Short yet obese, he staggers like a drunk and has vomit on his white England football shirt and hi-vis vest. But he's bleeding, too. Or there's blood on him. Plenty of it, in fact: on his hardhat, his forehead, his forearms, his hands. Most troubling, though, is his eyes. Somehow, they're both bloodshot *and* cold.

Like he's possessed.

"Sir," Gurdeep says, a hand outstretched. "Are you okay? You know this area's been evacuated?"

He ain't listenin'.

The fellow isn't stopping either. He's walking faster, his legs shaking, head lolling from left to right rhythmically, teeth shivering.

And now there's another, a woman. She's as scrawny as the man is fat, and she moves towards the yard with more purpose.

Dey ain't stoppin'.

Chapter 34 — Theo Callaghan — 10:25

You are the biggest pussy ever, Callaghan.

He escaped death by climbing through a ground floor window shattered by the drone's guns. He's been in Gabriela's tower block for nearly five hours. Yet he only started searching for his friend half an hour ago. Plus he's been going so slowly, so cautiously – pausing and cowering every time he hears the slightest movement elsewhere in the building – that he's cleared one solitary storey. And why?

Because yer a chicken-shit pussy. No wonder Devon Atkinson bullies ya. No wonder Gabriela friend-zoned ya.

Devon's probably dead now, eaten, undead or blown to pieces by the death-dealing machines flying around Walkley. He's big for a thirteen year-old, and he's probably the least intelligent boy in their age group. Gabriela, though, is smart; she may well be alive. But Theo will never find out at this rate.

Need t' be quicker. She could be dyin' somewhere, or in danger. Zombies could get 'ere soon, or perhaps there are drones that can go inside buildings.

With this in mind, he takes the stairs to the first floor. Like the one beneath, all of its apartment doors are open. It must be some kind of security measure. Forcing himself to move with more urgency, Theo investigates two flats and finds nothing but scattered clothes, spilt drinks and overturned furniture. The third place has a trail of blood leading from the kitchen to the bedroom and a pool of puke in the bathroom sink.

Where are all the dead bodies? Why's it not like my street, crawlin' wi' undead cannibals?

There's nothing of note in the rest of the second storey's residences. Signs of unrest, maybe, but not chaos, not the hell found elsewhere in Walkley.

Passing an open window in the stairwell, he hears two newly-familiar sounds. Aeroplanes high above, spreading chemicals; UAVs much lower, spreading bullets. Both phenomena have perturbed him all morning. The latter more than the former, of course, due to the close encounter outside. But, he reflects as he enters 201 Great Bear House, the planes might be just as dangerous. The trails they leave could well be causing people to transform into zombies. As for the death-drones, they're as much of a mystery. UK Armed Forces have used them for years, and according to the Internet, the machines are becoming increasingly powerful.

Can't be the British Army, though. They wouldn't be tryin' t' kill innocent kids like me, 'cause they're the good guys. The 'terrorist' rumours must be right. Some foreign country's got it in fer us, again, 'n' they've hacked into our defences, 'n' they're usin' our own weapons against us.

It's the only explanation that makes sense.

He finds nobody on the second floor, though in 212 there's an old, dead woman sat in her armchair. There's no sign of foul play; she could've died of natural causes. Either way, she smells bad, so Theo continues his mission. If he remembers correctly – and he should, because he replays conversations with Gabriel in his mind every night – her residence is on the seventh floor. But she has friends and an aunt elsewhere in the building, hence why he's being thorough.

Must be a pain in the arse livin' in a tower block.

She often complains that the lifts are broke. Which means she has to go up and down all of these stairs on a frequent basis. It's no wonder she's so slim. The elevators aren't in operation at the moment either, probably due to some emergency protocol. As he concludes another fruitless floor search and goes up to the fourth floor, Theo's already tiring.

Need to get buff, get fit. Work out. Start joggin' again instead o' playin' PlayStation every evenin' 'n' weekend. Maybe Gabriela'll date me then —

A bump above. Not 5th, higher up, 6th or 7th perhaps. Just about to exit the stairway and check 4th, Theo freezes. He listens. Is it the undead? No, he can hear voices. Male ones, deep enough to carry through the walls. Someone laughs. Then there's a smashing sound. Glass breaks; wood splinters. Another bray of laughter.

Who are they? Don't they know we're in the apocalypse?

Although Theo's gut tells him to run back downstairs and take his chances in the open, he refuses to listen. He's been too much of a coward over the last twelve hours. It's time to man up. If the men upstairs are here for nefarious reasons, he needs to help Gabriela, not abandon her. Therefore, he takes a big gulp, rolls his shoulders and heads for 401.

Again, he finds nothing. Not until he reaches 409, at least: its sole occupant is as deceased as the elderly lady in 212. This time there's blood, a pool of the stuff. More than enough to imply that the scrawny dead man spread-eagled on the filthy kitchen floor has been murdered.

With a hand over his mouth, Theo edges towards the corpse. He has to step over numerous magazines and newspapers. Those closest to body are splashed crimson, as is the linoleum. A putrid reek is getting sharper, worsening his nausea, though it's not clear if it's coming from the unfortunate resident or the pile of dishes in the sink.

The boy expects to find awful bite wounds to the fellow's neck or face. He's underwhelmed by the head injury, which looks like the flat occupant's banged his head hard. *Not zombies.*

In the lounge, on a coffee table stained by dozen of cup ring marks, there's a tablet, into which is plugged a pair of leopard-print headphones. The mobile device is protected by a case adorned with purple butterflies.

Another bump from above. *Perhaps they're looters, or somethin', 'n' this ol' guy tried t' fight back.*

Then there's a screech, that of a young girl.

Chills run down Theo's spine. He leaves the dead body, hurries out of the flat and runs to the stairs. As the stairwell door closes behind him, he hears one open over his head. He tries to reopen the door without being detected. But he's not quick enough. Someone shouts. The kid looks up to see, two stories up, a gang of five or six young men. He recognises one who's at least ten years older than the rest. Danny Rowbottom. *With a fuckin' gun in his hand.*

Taking two steps at a time, Theo rushes down the stairs. Boots and shoes beat a terrifying tempo above. Insults and threats are yelled. He's quicker than them, though; they're getting in each other's way. Before long, he's en route from 1st to ground. *I'll come back for Gabriela. Get rid o' these dickheads 'n' come back when the coast's clear.*

He's on the mezzanine, about to descend the final flight, when the ground floor stairwell door opens. An arm appears, its hand covered in dry blood, the sleeve torn to rags. Then a barefooted leg.

Theo's seen enough. He turns tail and bolts back up the stairs. The footfalls beneath him are slower, more deliberate than Rowbottom's gang's, but a quick glance down the central shaft indicates there's at least seven, maybe nine of the fiends. He reaches the first floor just as Rowbottom's swiftest minion appears on the mezzanine between 1st and 2nd.

"Oi!" the baseball bat-wielding skinhead grunts. "Come 'ere, ya little shit!"

Ignoring the lout, Theo opens the stairway exit door and runs.

He's gone no more than five paces when he hears the first scream. And it's not the last. As he tiptoes away from the battle between chavs and zombies, he can't help but listen to the carnage. Shouts of panic are soon shouts of terror, then agony. Most are cut off mid-breath. More disturbing are the wet sounds, like wellington boots in thick mud.

Rowbottom's handgun discharges five times, and the feared local gangster even roars in defiance. Perhaps his weapon buys him time to escape; footsteps echo through the tower walls for a moment. Then there's a silence, which is almost as frightening as the racket it follows.

Still creeping, ears straining for signs of pursuit, Theo carries on down the corridor. He follows the U-shaped passage to its conclusion, where he finds the high-rise's south staircase. It was locked at ground floor level. He's been reluctant to check it since, preferring to stick to the known quantity, the north stairs. Now he has no choice.

His final resort is a non-starter. It's not locked, but there appears to be an obstruction on the other side. The door won't budge.

Unlike its opposite number to the south. Even from this distance, one side of the tower to the other, Theo knows the clatter of metal door slammed into plaster wall spells bad news.

Find somewhere t' hide. Now.

He tries to ignore the bile rising in his throat and a sudden cramp in his bowels. *Think, dickhead, think. You've checked all these apartments. Which one looked the best to 'ide in?*

The boy knows he needs to focus. He's paralysed, though, like a field mouse beneath a diving owl. Except there's no avian screech freezing his faculties; it's the steady, labouring plods of two or three walking dead turning his legs to lead and mind to mush.

Focus, Callaghan!

Apartment 115 – or 116, no 115 – that's where he needs to go. He sprints, reaching the bend to the left just as a male zombie rounds the opposite corner. Its arms, one of them ending in a bloody stump, shoot out; its legs accelerate. As Theo slips into 115, a female freak stumbles into view.

Two of 'em. Rowbottom 'n' 'is crew did good.

Straight to the kitchen he goes. The open toolbox is still there, on the pan-cluttered counter. He takes a hammer and a flat-blade screwdriver and retreats to the hallway. Once he's shut and latched the front door, he enters the bathroom and locks himself in.

The pair of monsters take all of ten minutes to break in. Almost immediately, they assault the bathroom door. Theo stands, trembling, his bladder aching, vision pulsing red, makeshift weapons ready.

MDF shatters, and the male zombie piles into the room. Mustering all of his strength, the boy smashes it in the face with the hammer, so hard he drops the tool. The fiend spins like a top and tumbles into the female zomb, which reels away, falls and lands on its back. Without a moment's hesitation, Theo drops to one knee and buries the screwdriver in its eye. It sticks; he can't get it loose and doesn't have time to keep trying.

He's rising to his feet when hands grasp at his back. Gasping, he scrambles away but something strong grabs his right calf. He stumbles. Kicks back with left foot. The grip on his leg slackens. Now he's crawling. Out of the bathroom. Hears steps from the main corridor so goes right towards the kitchen. He needs to get another tool, the chisel or mallet, perhaps.

Zombie number three's in the apartment now. In his haste, Theo trips over a cardboard box. As he goes to the ground, he twists to face the new threat.

But there is no third zombie. It's Gabriela, beautiful, blood-spattered Gabriela Popescu. She has a crowbar in her hands and a fearsome look on her face.

Chapter 35 — Jada Blakowska — 11:35

"No, we don't *know* it won't fire." She massages the bridge of her nose. "But how long have we been here now?"

Brad shrugs. "An hour? Hour fifteen?"

"Long enough t' lose any chance o' findin' Connor 'n' Evie," Luke says bitterly.

Brad shoots him an evil look. "What the fuck we supposed t' do, bro? Walk out there 'n' get shot t' pieces by that drone motherfucker?"

Jada winces. *Gonna be trouble between those two.* The filling station kiosk is warm, claustrophobic and sour-smelling; the atmosphere is charged.

"Beats stayin' 'ere 'n' gettin' blown up. All it 'as t' do is shoot one o' the petrol pumps 'n' *boom!* That's us outta the game fer good."

"But it *won't fire*. Whoever's controllin' it obviously doesn't wanna do that much damage —"

"Are you takin' the piss? The final missile, last night, landed 'alf a mile from 'ere! They destroyed the whole fuckin' town, fer fucksake. 'N' ya reckon that drone's 'oldin' off 'cause it don't wanna waste one little petrol station?"

Crushing an empty cola can in his hand, Brad shakes his head. "Ya saw 'ow powerful that drone was. Blew the milk float t' shit in —"

"— Yeah," Luke interjects, "a fuckin' milk float, not a —"

"— So? Ya not think it'll splatter our guts all over the place? Unlike you, mate, I ain't got no deathwish —"

"— The fuck ya talkin' about? I don't wanna die. I just wanna save —"

"— Yer kid. As if we're gonna forget."

"The fuck's *that* supposed to mean?"

"All ya fuckin' go on about is yer kid. I lost mine, bro." Brad's voice breaks, but he clears his throat. "'Ad t' kill 'er meself. Just a few hours ago. 'N' I gotta listen t' you goin' on about Connor non-fuckin'-stop!"

Luke closes his eyes. "Shit, mate, I'm sorry. I just feel like such a shit dad —"

"'N' off ya go again! 'Shit, mate, I'm sorry'… then ya just start talkin' 'bout yerself, 'n' *your* fuckin' problems again."

"Pardon me fer bein' concerned 'bout my son missin' in a town full o' fuckin' zombies!"

"If ya were *that* fuckin' concerned, ya woulda kept yer eye on 'im. No way LaRosa woulda got away from me —"

"You fuckin' what?" Luke starts towards his friend. "Fuckin' say that again, ya prick!"

Brad throws his arms wide. "What ya gonna do, asshole?"

"Guys, guys!" Jada's been staring out of the window, watching the drone hovering, sipping coffee. Now, arms folded, she turns to face her bickering friends with a withering gaze. "Calm down, both o' you. You're like a pair o' kids." *Jeez. I sound like my mum.* "This arguing is gettin' us nowhere. Let's talk about what we're doin' next."

The two men quail under her gaze and return to glowering at each other.

"Come on! We can't stay in here forever. For all we know, that drone's operator's gone home sick. Someone could come and replace him, and blow us to hell —"

"— Pretty sure they're automated," chimes Brad. "Was watchin' this vid —"

"— Okay, whatever. The fact remains that we have multiple reasons to make a move, quick. So let's start thinkin' of a way out."

"What's the fuckin' point?" Luke stares at his scuffed shoes. "Let 'em blow us up."

"Luke, don't be ridiculous. Gould's lost track of Connor, but he's doin' his best, an' I'm sure he'll find 'em again. We need to be ready for when he does."

"'Ave *you* got any suggestions?" Brad opens a chocolate bar wrapper and eats the snack in two bites.

"Take that bastard on."

"We're all low on ammo." Luke pushes himself off the counter and, crunching bags of crisps and sweets underfoot, walks as close to the shop front as he dares. "'N' that thing's too fast."

"Fast, maybe, but smart?"

The men shrug.

"I don't think so. We're smarter. Or *I* am, at least. Maybe not you two, wastin' our time arguin' like testosterone-pumped schoolboys."

They smile dutifully.

"I get the feelin' that drone isn't bothered about us in particular. What d'ya reckon, Brad? You've seen videos about 'em, you said."

"Hunter/Killers." Brad cocks his head to one side. "That's what the survivalists call 'em, anyway. They latch onto targets till a better target comes along. I'm not even sure that's the same type, like, the one outside. Could be —"

"— Could be different, yeah." Jada turns and faces the ugly machine again. It's not moved a millimetre. "But let's just work with what little we do know. Better targets, you say? Like, it'll switch?"

"Yeah."

"So we distract it. We don't change the narrative, because we can't. We're stuck in here. Instead, we create a *new* narrative."

"We're not writin' newspapers, Jada," Luke warns. "We're tryin' to escape a flyin' killer-robot."

"Same principle. The drone is a media consumer. We want it to forget something, so we do that by drawin' its attention to something else. 'Cause it won't forget us otherwise."

Brad makes a face. "I dunno. Reckon we should just try 'n' shoot it down. There's a window in the staff toilet, isn't there?"

"Yeah," says Luke. "It'll be a tough shot, but —"

"— And where do we shoot it, exactly?" Jada's eyebrows raise. "Looks like it's covered in armour. We have two pistols and a glorified machine-pistol, all low calibre. Plus a shotgun, which won't be worth shit at this range."

"If we shoot it enough times…" Luke looks as doubtful as he sounds.

"Eight shotgun shells. Twenty-seven rounds for the MP5. The pea-shooters have about a dozen rounds each. We could use all of 'em without puttin' a dent in it."

Brad's nodding. "Video I saw, the Hunter/Killer was vulnerable to assault rifle fire and above."

"There you go, then. So we do it my way."

They nod their acquiescence; she explains her plan. Using a stolen disposable lighter, lighter fluid and emptied candy bar boxes, they start a fire. Almost immediately, an alarm is triggered. The group cover their ears and wait. Five minutes pass, and nothing happens. Intent on the petrol station forecourt and Cenotaph Street beyond, Jada strives to ignore the pessimistic mutterings and facial expressions of the males.

She turns around after ten minutes and allows herself a sigh. "Okay, fair enough. So we shoot it —"

"Zombie!" Brad erupts.

"Two!" Luke points.

The two ghouls, both males wearing biker gear, are on Cenotaph.

The drone's moving, which is their cue to do likewise. Jada flies through the door as the UAV's cannon fires its first volley. As arranged, she goes right. Then around the back of the garage, into a back alley. The gun yammers again. Concrete splinters in her wake as high-velocity rounds riddle the building wall, almost drowning out the shrill fire alarm.

Luke and Brad appear ahead – they went the opposite way around.

All three almost collide with the twenty foot fence bordering the alleyway. They begin to climb, desperate to reach the factory car park beyond.

The drone's gun fires. Then once more, but from a different direction.

"Reinforcements!" Brad, the quickest, is at the top of the fence. He points to the sky; a second UAV is about fifty yards from the first.

Jada reaches the summit second. The smattering of zombies surrounding the petrol station is becoming a horde. Inevitably, some wander around the back of the kiosk. The fleetest grasps at Luke's foot and gets a kick in the face for its trouble.

After climbing most of the way down, Jada copies Brad and drops the last few feet, wincing at the pain in her still-swollen ankle. She flinches, for some of the undead are reaching between the railings. Others are starting to scale the fence. Meanwhile, the hum of a drone is getting closer.

Across the parking lot they go, intent on reaching the plastic processing plant. It'll give them cover from the drones. While the zombies are trying to break in, they'll be torn to shreds by cannon-fire. Then the humans can escape. Unlike the gas station, the factory will have multiple exits. They've already radioed Gould to tell him their plan, and he's advised them to enter via an open door at the southwestern of the plant.

They're over halfway across the lot when Jada risks a look over her shoulder: the first zombies are conquering the fence. The fiends don't climb down. They simply throw themselves to the ground, landing with slaps and cracks.

"Come on!" Brad yells. Far more athletic than the other two, he reaches the factory wall at least fifteen yards earlier than the others. He uses his pistol to snipe the fastest of the zombies while holding a fire door open. Luke crosses the threshold first, then turns and adds his own gunfire to Brad's. Once Jada's through, the door is slammed shut.

They're at the end of a gloomy corridor. The first door on the right leads to an office, from which they drag a filing cabinet. After they've pushed it and a water cooler in front of the fire exit, they work their way through the industrial unit. Their footsteps ring loud down long corridors, though every few seconds, cannon-fire outside drowns out any other noise. The smell of chemicals is strong enough to wrinkle Jada's nose.

"Gould?" Luke says into the radio. "D'ya read me? Over."

"Loud and clear. Over." The transport manager sounds bored.

"Any sign o' the kids? Over."

"No. Still working on it. You made it into the plastic place? Over."

"Yeah. Have ya got access to their cameras yet? Over."

"Yes. Just now. Few bodies here 'n' there, but providing none of them start moving, you'll be alright. Over."

"Which exit's lookin' best?" Jada asks.

"Hang on…" Gould clicks his tongue. "North east corner, looks like. That should keep you outta the drones' lines of sight. Over."

"As long as they don't move," pants Brad.

"Over!" barks Gould. "Don't forget to say 'over'. But yes, as you say, as long as the drones don't move. I think they're having too much fun, though. Over."

Jada frowns. "Whaddya mean, too much fun? Over."

"Well, we're talking a really big horde in the car park now. Over."

Luke gulps. "'Ow big? Over."

"Few hundred. Over."

Jada, Luke and Brad stop for a moment, and all three lean on the walls to catch their breath. They're in a corridor in the administrative wing of the establishment.

"Shit," says the former, downcast. "An' I thought I was bein' clever, startin' that alarm to get us outta the garage."

"Well," says Brad, "it's not like we 'ad any better ideas, is it?"

"Still reckon we coulda shot it down…" Luke half-smiles. "Okay, I'm just shittin' you."

"Guys?" Gould's voice crackles. "Are you still moving towards that exit? Over."

Shit. We're standin' 'round, chattin.' Need to sharpen up. Jada starts to walk again. "Yeah, why? Over."

"We've got zombies showing up on that side. Do not exit the factory. Repeat, do not exit the factory. Over."

Chapter 36 — Luke Norman — 11:55

Now we're stuck in this fuckin' factory. 'N' Connor's out there, probably dead by now.

Brad's always been blunt, sometimes painfully so, but he was right when he blamed his friend for losing Connor. As was his ex, the boy's mum, when she labelled him irresponsible and selfish. He was understandably tired on the bus, but by succumbing to sleep, he was putting himself first. Dismissing his son's desire to find his mum was ill-advised. And now they're both paying for his shortcomings.

I don't deserve to 'ave kids. 'N' Connor deserves better than me. It shoulda been 'is mum 'n' Trent who survived —

"Luke?" Jada calls from outside the toilet cubicle. "Whatever you're doin' in there, we don't have time for it. The factory is pretty much surrounded. Every door's locked apart from the one we came in. Drones both sides. But even so —"

"Okay, okay." *Get a grip, Norman. Ya need t' survive this 'n' rescue yer lad. Not cower away in 'ere like a beaten dog.*

He spits the final remains of bile from his mouth and pushes himself away from the toilet bowl. As he stands, he wobbles. Lack of food was already weakening him, and vomiting hasn't helped. The sound of banging on the building's walls sets his pulse racing; a welcome burst of adrenaline gets him going.

"You okay?" Jada asks as he emerges from the stall.

He's only been in there for a minute, but he feels silly for losing his composure at such a crucial juncture. "Yeah. Been better, but I'll survive."

"Hopefully. You have…"

He wipes a smear of puke from the corner of his mouth. "Ugh. Sorry 'bout that."

"Never mind. Come on. Brad's already got to work."

The bathroom's around the corner from the aforementioned entrance. As promised, Brad's busy moving office furniture in front of the door. "Y'alright, bro?"

"Yeah." *Whole thing wi' Connor literally worryin' me sick, but I won't risk another row by mentionin' it again.* "I'm good. What's the plan?"

"Yer lookin' at it. We block the door. We fight any that get through. Then we dust."

"What about the drones?"

Jada winces; Brad shrugs.

"We need t' find a vehicle. Don't matter if it's noisy, 'cause the drones'll catch us even if it's not. So it just needs t' be fast."

The smashing of glass has them looking towards the barricade. Although obstructions block the view, it's clear the zombies on the attack have breached the door and are now free to assault the pile of fixtures and fittings. Bangs and knocks echo through the factory walls as the invaders attempt to gain access elsewhere. Outside, UAV cannons rain fire on the undead yet to find the unlocked door.

"The other entrances are pretty secure, right?" says Luke.

"I guess so." Brad wipes sweat from his face. "They're locked, at least, which makes 'em better than this one."

"But zombies can break through locked doors, can't they? Given enough time."

"Yeah." Jada puffs her cheeks. "But what else can we do? I just wish I'd never come up with that stupid 'attract the zombies to distract the drones' idea. Now we've got both of 'em on our case."

As if to confirm, a sustained barrage of drone fire roars directly above.

"Y'know what, Jada…" Luke bites his top lip. He stares at the corridor's walls without seeing the signs or posters.

"What, Luke?" she asks, frowning.

"It actually wasn't that bad of an idea." He grins when her eyes narrow. "Not bein' patronisin', or anythin' —"

"— Ya kinda are, bro," Brad says, peering through a gap in the debris keeping the monsters at bay.

"No, ya don't understand." *So fuckin' explain it to 'em 'n' stop wastin' time!* "The fire alarm got us outta a shitty situation then. Attracted zombies to distract drones. It was the right call at that point. But now, we've got the opposite problem. Trapped by zombies rather than drones."

"So? Get to the point, Luke," Jada urges.

"'Ang on. Let me just speak to Gould." He holds up a hand to deter any protests. "Gould? Do you read me? Over."

"Loud and clear, over."

"Can ya get a view o' the factory? From outside, like?"

The tech-wiz clicks his tongue. "Give me a sec... here we go. Reasonable view from the eastern side. Looks like you've got your hands full there! Don't think I've ever seen that many in one place —"

"— What about drones?"

"Still three o' them. One's not doing much, though. Maybe it's out of ammo. Other two are still firing away, but there are so many zombies, they're barely making a dent. Over."

"Thanks. Any sign o' Connor?"

"Not recently. I'll keep you posted, though, over."

"Okay. Over."

Both Jada and Brad are now watching the enemies at the door. "If you're comin' up with a plan, Luke," the former says, "I suggest you hurry."

"Gonna 'ave t' make a move soon," Brad adds. "This blockage ain't gonna keep 'em out much longer."

"So we'll block it some more." Luke leads the way, heading to the closest storage room, which has a stronger chemical smell and is full of barrels. They pick one each and begin to roll them back to the main corridor. Once he's positioned his against a filing cabinet, Luke takes a breath. "We need t' follow Jada's plan again, but this time we need t' attract drones, not zombies."

"'N 'ow do we do that?" Brad's already on his way back to the store room. "They don't seem t' be overly-bothered by the fire alarm, or the 'undreds o' zombies outside, do they?"

Jada's close behind. "Attack *them*. The drones, I mean. They *did* respond to the fire alarm, or maybe it was to the zombie horde. Not in any great number, but they reacted. So if we attack them directly…"

"'Ow, though?" Luke grimaces as he grabs a second barrel; the injuries incurred the previous day are niggling. "We can't open or smash windows without lettin' those ugly freaks in!"

Brad stops short, letting his barrel roll down the corridor. "The roof."

"Too exposed," Luke contends.

"We're gonna be pretty exposed down here, soon!" Jada has to raise her voice over the din of zombies battering and crunching their way towards lunch. "Half o' this barricade is gone now."

"Fuck it, then," says Luke.

They find a staircase within a couple of minutes. Access to the roof – above the second floor – is denied by a locked door, but Brad's axe makes light work of the padlock and chain. Tentatively, with Jada leading the way, they step out into the sunshine.

Luke covers his mouth and nose. The stench of at least a thousand day-old carcasses is chastening; the roof door is only ten yards from the closest ledge. He and his friends turn standing circles, scouring the sky for UAVs.

"There!" Brad points: a black drone swoops from north to south, its gun blazing.

Ten seconds later, Brad spots the second. It's higher, at least 150ft from the ground, and its cannon is silent.

"That's the one outta ammo," Luke surmises. "We should target that one."

Jada's still searching. She moves a little closer to the edge to see past an exhaust vent. "Should be one more, remember. We need to know where they all are before we start shootin'."

A sudden whirring, buzzing noise has her and the men scrambling for cover. Rising like a cobra's head from a snake charmer's pot, the third drone emerges from beneath the parapet. It pauses for a moment, just a few yards away.

Is it outta ammo too?

The cannon is painfully loud up close. Throwing himself flat, Luke prays for salvation.

Suddenly, sparks are flying from the machine's metal hide. Luke glances left: Jada is on her belly, firing her SMG. So he draws the two pistols and all but empties their clips, aiming at the squat, thick gun under the UAV's nose. Meanwhile, Brad's unloading with his shotgun.

The cannon sags. Its barrel swings down as if it's aiming at the ground. Now the drone simply hovers, almost malevolent in its stillness.

"Quick, inside!" Jada yells.

Back in the building, Luke buzzes Gould while Jada and Brad search the second floor's closest rooms for something to block the stairwell. "Gould? Over." He takes a deep breath. The chemical smell is offensive, but it's better than the miasma of rotting dead people.

The older man, who for once doesn't sound like he's half-asleep, takes a moment to reply. "I read you, Luke. Was just about to contact you, over."

"Yeah? Anyway, keep an eye on the outdoor camera 'ere. We reckon, or we 'ope there'll be drones on the way. Over."

"Roger that. Good news, by the way. I've found Connor and Evie —"

"— No shit! Where?"

"You're supposed to wait till I say 'over' before you speak, Luke. Over."

"Sorry. Where were they? Over."

"Where *are* they, you mean. Ashara's keeping watch on them as we speak. They're on the edge of Mortborough. Not far from that hotel your dead paedophile friend owned. Over."

"Awesome!" Luke looks down the stairs; Brad and Jada are positioning crates and racks on the mezzanine between the first and second floors. "He wasn't my friend, though. Anyway, as soon as the drones arrive, we'll go. Over"

"*If* they arrive," Gould snaps. "In fact… you might be in luck, over."

"Why? Over."

"False alarm, sorry. Thought I saw more drones heading your way, but I had my camera feeds mixed up —"

All of a sudden, there's a massive bang. Followed almost instantaneously by a second. Gould's voice stops. Or maybe not; Luke doesn't know because he's not holding the walkie-talkie anymore, and even if he were, his hearing has gone. He's not even standing. He can only see smoke and dust. Plus, if he squints, the outline of a door. Daylight. His back hurts from the steps digging into his torso.

What the fuck?

"Guys?" he calls. Luke can't hear his own voice. In fact, his speech is audible, but only as an echo. "Guys, where are you?"

"Down 'ere!" Brad must be at least a hundred yards away.

"Me too!" Jada sounds in pain.

"'Eadin' your way," Brad calls.

Abruptly, they're before him, seizing him by the forearms and pulling him upright. *'Ow did they get 'ere so quick?*

Coughing, Luke opens the roof door. He shields his eyes from the sun and stumbles into the open. The reek of undead is all but gone, scoured clear by fire and ash.

"Don't worry," says Brad, right behind him. "I grabbed the radio."

"Keep an eye open for drones." Jada walks past the two men towards the edge of the roof, which is now a few yards closer. A good-sized slice of the building has been reduced to rubble. "Jesus Christ."

Luke joins her. He mops grit and grime from his eyes with the hem of his shirt and struggles to comprehend the destruction below. Hundreds of zombies are in thousands of blackened, steaming pieces. There's a crater in the centre of the car park, with mangled vans and cars in flames. The drones have disappeared. "So that's what 'appens when ya shoot up a drone."

"Maybe." Brad scratches his head, sending a shower of dust from his newly-grey hair. "Or maybe they were just respondin' to the horde. Anyway, we better go. It's clear this side, but fer 'ow long?"

Jada's already heading back inside. "The factory'll have absorbed a lot of the blast. Zombies on the other side'll be fine."

Damage to the plastic plant's walls gives the trio an easy exit. The fence over which they climbed earlier is in ruins, so they're soon back at the filling station. Or what's left of it, at least. Debris from the missile strike must've hit something flammable, because the kiosk is a smouldering ruin, while the petrol pumps have vanished entirely. Black smoke streams into the air; visibility is poor.

"Some o' the zombs were bikers." Brad splutters due to the acrid fumes.

Luke blinks away tears. "There's a bike!"

There are at least twenty motorcycles lined up in a lay-by near the garage. Some have been overturned by the fuel explosion's shockwave, and most don't have keys in the ignition. But before long, Luke, Jada and Brad sit astride vintage choppers, speeding westwards. Gould's lost track of the kids; they've gone into an area with inoperative cameras. *They can't 'ave gone far, though, can they? We'll be there in a coupla minutes.*

With the wind on his face, tired arms invigorated by the bike's feedback, Luke feels hope for the first time in hours. He rides quickest. Like a man possessed. Dodging broken-down cars and craters. Accelerating on straights, decelerating as little as he dares at bends.

Before long, they're entering Mortborough. The crumbling, devastated remains of his hometown's outskirts should depress him; they don't. All that matters is the boy. *Just one more block… another hundred yards… then a left…*

Except they don't even need to make the turn.

At the next junction. On the corner. Two bicycles, blue and purple, are lay on their sides, pedals pointing at the sky. Connor and Evie are nowhere to be seen.

Chapter 37 — Floyd Nelson — 12:40

Dey ain't as bad-ass as dey look.

That's what he keeps telling himself. And that's what he keeps proving to himself, too, because every time one of the gruesome fiends appears, he shoots it in the head. They're not armed; they're not organised; they have zero intelligence. Against trained soldiers, attacking in twos and threes, they're more of an irritant than a threat. Still, both Floyd and Gurdeep – the latter more so, admittedly – find themselves dry-mouthed and shaky-handed whenever the crazed men and women appear.

"'Ow long should we stay?" asks Gurdeep. Like his squadmate, he's using the water feature wall as a rest for his rifle.

"Dunno, fam." Floyd mops sweat from his brow. He spits into the pool and watches as his saliva is assimilated into bubbles from the cascade spewed by the ornamental stone volcano. Sniffing the air, he scents corrupting flesh and something more synthetic. *Probably whatever dem airplanes are dumpin' all ova da gaffe.* "We leave da kids, 'n' dey're as good as dead. Can't take dem wiv us, eiva."

Said children are Bonnie, Rufus and Jimmy. Currently, they're in the bandstand at the rear of the park's botanical gardens. They're safe, for the only entry to this section is guarded by two British Army soldiers. For now.

Slaying the hostiles at Swinford Industrial Estate proved easy – once they overcame the initial shock of encountering horror movie bad guys in real life. A large mob tried to stop them leaving the area, but an air strike saved the day. The privates went west, until they heard children screaming in the park at the border with Walkley. Still disconnected from army comms, there was no choice to make. They've been defending the youngsters for the last couple of hours.

"Why d'ya fink they keep comin'?" Gurdeep wonders, having just shot another of the psychos.

"Dunno, fam." Floyd rolls his neck, which clicks with tension. "Maybe we picked da wrong place to hole up."

"What, like this is where they wanna be, 'n' we're gettin' in the way?"

"Maybe. Who knows? I didn't even know dey were a ting till two hours ago."

"The officers'll probably know more, innit. Shit rolls downhill, so we'll learn the script after every other fucker. Your headset still dead?"

"Yeah. Just dat annoyin' buzz. No orders means we just do what seems right, ya get me?"

Gurdeep makes a show of checking his ammunition supply. "'Ow long will we last, though? Eh? If most people in these shitty towns 'ave turned into these… things, we're talkin', what? 'Undred thousand? Million?"

"Depends 'ow much it's spread." Floyd hears children's voices getting louder. "Dem planes… dey're probably sprayin' some sorta antidote."

"Antidote to what, though?"

"Dere's sometin' in da air, fam. Dem inhalers dey gave us, dat's our vaccination."

"So what about the kids, then? Why 'aven't they turned?"

"Maybe dey got given da inhalers too. We should ask dem."

Floyd's about to head to the bandstand when another gang of zombies arrives. They're despatched as swiftly as their predecessors, with Floyd killing seven to Gurdeep's four. They've been keeping count; the former has notched twice as many as his mate.

"Right, I'll go 'n' speak to dem youts. Make sure dey're still behavin' demselves, too —" His comm unit beeps, as does Gurdeep's.

"Privates Singh and Nelson? Over." Lieutenant Pirie's educated voice invokes both hope and fear.

"Yes, sir," both reply.

"Report. Over."

"Ah… sir?" Singh stutters.

"We've been off da grid, sir," Nelson cuts in. "Comms dead —"

"— We know. Just a technical issue —"

"— 'N' zombies, sir!" Singh blurts.

"Zombies? Repeat, over."

"Hostiles, sir," Nelson clarifies. "Behavin' very strangely, sir. Over."

"You're gonna need to do better than that, Nelson. 'Strangely' how? Over."

Between them, the soldiers elaborate.

Pirie pauses for a moment when they're done. "Privates?"

"Sir?"

"I need you both to shut up for a moment. Okay? Over."

They acquiesce.

"I have someone with me, an Agent Randall Maguire, from MI6. He will be briefing you. Over."

Neither private responds; they share a bemused look.

"Privates? Good to speak to you, over." Maguire's accent is faintly Irish.

"Sir?" both reply.

"So here's how this is gonna play, boys. First of all, there are no 'zombies'. Okay? This isn't Hollywood. I wish it was. It'd be easier to deal with a load of flesh-eating, mindless monsters —"

"Sir," Floyd interjects, "I've personally shot 'n' killed twenty-two o' dese tings. Dey ain't human, sir. Dere's sometin very unusual —"

"— An' that's exactly where we're goin' wrong, Private Nelson. That kinda thinkin's gonna get you both killed —"

"— Apologies, sir, just tellin' it like it is. Over."

"That's just your *perception* of how it is, Private. Over."

It's my perception, 'cause dat's what's 'appened.

"So what exactly should we 'ave perceived, sir?" Gurdeep asks.

The agent chuckles. "That's the sorta question that'll take you a long way, Private. Okay, let's try again. You haven't encountered any *zombies*. These guys you've been shootin', they may have been scary customers. They may look like they're about to jump on you an' start feedin' on your brains. But that's not the truth, I promise you."

Floyd scowls. He surreptitiously tries to get his friend's attention, but the Asian refuses to meet his eye. *Good-lookin' but dumb, dat guy.*

"The truth," Maguire continues, "is just as we've suspected all along. We're dealin' with terrorists. But not your average, garden-variety, 'Allahu Akbar' nutjobs. We're talkin' sophisticated. We're talkin' creative. We're talking large scale, more of an insurrection than a terror attack. This 'zombie' effect you mention… that's all it is, an effect. An illusion that —"

"Sir," Floyd begins, "dey seemed realistic. Wasn't no CGI FX —"

"Private Nelson," Pirie barks. "Don't interrupt the man. There's too much info to waste time. And Agent Maguire is the lead here now, so you'll treat him like he's a fucking general, you hear? No more interruptions. Over."

"Of course, sir. Sorry, sir. Over."

"No worries, Nelson." Maguire's tone remains genial. "Let's simplify this a little. You two now have three clear directives. One, you enforce evacuation. If you see any civilians who haven't been radicalised, you order them to leave the area and head to Manchester city centre."

Floyd and Nelson share another pregnant look. The wind is picking up now, and the smells of burning and decaying flesh are strengthening. Dead plants rustle against each other; birds call in the air.

"Two. Any civvies who disobey your order to disperse and vacate, you will shoot on sight. They are part of the insurrection, and they will be dangerous. They will possibly even attack before you give them chance to comply."

Ignoring Gurdeep's warning stare, Floyd clears his throat. "Permission to speak, sir? Over."

The lieutenant sounds ready to deny, but Maguire says, "Go ahead, Nelson."

"We shoot dese civvies, da ones who don't listen, right?"

"Right, Private."

"'Cause dey dangerous, right?"

"Yes."

"But what about kids? If dey refuse to leave, we kill dem too?"

"Unfortunately, yes. Drastic times call for drastic measures."

"But 'ow can kids be 'insurrectionists', sir? Don't make no sense."

"Private Nelson," Pirie growls. "You are a soldier. You follow orders. You don't ask questions. If MI6 say they're insurrectionary terrorists, they're insurrectionary terrorists. Do you understand, over?"

"Wilco, sir. Over." *Dis is buuuuulllllshit. Man's killin' no youts, ya get me?* He shakes his head; Gurdeep's biting his top lip.

"Thank you, Lieutenant." Maguire is as unflustered as ever. "Which leads me onto directive three. Checkin' your location, you're on the border between... ah… Swinford and Walkley, right? Over."

"Affirmative, sir," says Gurdeep; Floyd's lost in thought.

"Perfect. It turns out you two could be of some use to us. Now, before I go any further, understand that what I'm about to tell you is classified, at the highest level possible. Okay? Over."

"Yes, sir."

"We believe the person responsible for this insurrection is at large in the Mortborough area. We have a number of units in the area, but none as near as you, so they're not suitable for the task we're assigning to you —"

"— Which is what, sir?" asks Floyd. "Over."

"We need you to find one *Lena Adderley*. CEO of Evolve plc. You'll receive a photo and profile on your PDAs in the next few seconds. Get close to her. Tell her you've deserted 'cause you've been given orders you don't agree with. If she trusts you, great. You pump her for intel then terminate. If she doesn't, you terminate her immediately. Either way, as long as you stick to the script and she dies, you're home free. Mission accomplished, back to base."

While his friend nods, seemingly content, Floyd isn't so sure. "'N' what if we don't, sir? I mean, what if we fail? Over."

Footsteps fall nearby, on the main road accessing the park, probably. The squaddies stiffen.

"Failure is not an option, Private." Pirie's voice drips acid.

"You *won't* fail," Maguire adds. "You've both been recommended by your superiors. But… your lieutenant is correct."

One of the children yells something incoherent. Something panicked.

"If you do fail," Maguire continues, "we'll have to consider the overall picture. You guys disobeyed a direct order this mornin'. That on its own wouldn't land you in the shit, but added to a failure to deliver with Adderley… it doesn't look good, does it?"

Running feet nearby. Hands reach for guns. *But I'd rather face da zombies dan dese backstabbin' snakes.*

"Essentially, guys, you'll be treated as part o' the problem rather than part o' the solution. Over."

"I think you can read the subtext, fellas," Pirie sneers. "Over and out."

Chapter 38 — Lena Adderley — 12:45

Nine years ago, she and her beau stayed at the Pulitzer, Amsterdam. Opulent almost to a fault, the establishment was, and still is, regarded as one of the world's finest. That day, its clientele were shocked to learn that, in the early hours of the morning, one of the domestic staff had hanged himself. The barman wasn't found for several hours. Lena's boyfriend at the time, a vacuous professional footballer, was disquieted; she was unconcerned.

If she closes her eyes, she can almost feel the silk bed sheets on her skin. The chiselled thighs and abs of the Argentine star centre-forward, Santi Riciardo – a Manchester City player, so her United-supporting dad would've been disappointed had he found out – as they languished after a night of sweaty passion. Wiry, trimmed chest hair in her nostrils. The sportsman's rich, caramel voice and his stilted English. His musky scent offset by that of the previous evening's aftershave. His bass laugh. Delicious hors d'oeuvre in her mouth, washed down with the best champagne on offer.

Then she recalls other hotel stays, ones less luxurious, but equally as vivid in her memory. These recollections hurt, though, because they are of times spent with Harry Lunt. The big soldier was almost oafish when compared to Riciardo. But he was a gentle giant, his homicidal hands as tender as his kisses. Years later, last night, he came to her rescue. And she betrayed him with barely a second thought, because that's the kind of woman she is.

Imagine if Harry would've been at the Pulitzer. The posh snacks wouldn't have satisfied him. He would've ordered a 16oz steak and fries, with lager, no, ale, in his glass, not sparkling wine. The two of them would've had fun, laughed, joked. He wouldn't have been spooked by the dead bartender, either. He would've been as nonchalant as I was.

Today, the Evolve CEO is decidedly more perturbed by the prospect of sharing temporary accommodation with the dead. This place, on the outskirts of Mortborough is far from five stars. And there's not one deceased person here; there are three. The old woman, discovered amidst the ruins of a bed – which was probably on the first floor before missiles converted the place to into a half-roofed bungalow – passed away some time ago. The young boy and the nurse look to have been zombified at some point.

If only Harry was with me.

But he's not. He can't be, because I left him to die alone.

Parts of the wrecked building are sheltered from the merciless sun's rays. The temperature's almost as high as it was yesterday. The only smell is that of dust, which is thick enough to be tastable. Perhaps, by blocking out any other scent, this prevents passing zombies from sniffing out Lena. Or maybe pure chance keeps them at bay. Either way, she's reluctant to tempt fate. Because even if she can avoid the undead, there are soldiers in black uniforms on the ground and menacing drones on high.

The paramilitaries she encountered after escaping the van nearly killed her. Having chased her into a blood-spattered terraced house, they were about to flush her out when a mob of walking dead enjoined them in battle, and Lena used the distraction to flee. Before long, she came upon the bed and breakfast. Devastated by the air strike, it wasn't the most appealing of safe havens, but marauding zombies in the vicinity forced her inside.

Now this is my home. This grim house of the dead and undead.

She doesn't dare leave. Too many man-eating monsters, too many black-clad gunmen.

Perhaps this is what I deserve. No, there's no 'perhaps'. I directly caused deaths like the boy's and the nurse's. I indirectly caused all hell to rain down on these houses. No reason why I shouldn't have to hide here, in this half-exposed basement, wheezing with the dust, dead bodies over my head, fearing for my life but wanting to die...

Lena laughs to herself, and the noise is a pitiful croak. After all the destruction, she's only considering herself. The ruins and corpses should be a constant reminder of her narcissism, but self-pity dominates her thoughts.

What else is there to think about, though? Nothing. Everything has lost all meaning; everyone is gone. So she occupies her mind with the quandary that's distracted her from hunger, thirst, pain in her legs and despair for the last hour or so. She's been ignoring the reality that if she leaves the B&B, or even if she doesn't, cannibalistic freaks or special forces troops will snuff her out in moments. She's been pretending she has six choices.

One: commit suicide. Shamed businessmen the world over have jumped off bridges or put guns in their mouths over less. The guilt she feels is sufficiently painful to force her to take the ultimate medicine, and she doesn't envisage a future where she could ever forgive herself. However, she's also self-aware and knows she could never voluntarily take the final plunge into oblivion. No matter how much she wants or deserves such an end. Of course, soon enough, her life may be out of her hands. One confused zombie or curious black-ops fellow could easily find her; then she'll be dead, undead or captured and facing justice.

Two: leave, and never look back. This recourse is probably the most seductive. She wouldn't have to loop a noose around her own neck. Living a different life, in a new environment, she might eventually find peace of mind. Her disgrace would never be forgotten, and she would, no doubt, be reminded of her crimes on a frequent basis. A fresh start could be hers, though. Of course, she can't run faster than bullets. And how far would she have to go to be safe from the undead? Judging by the aeroplanes spraying chemicals from above, the authorities are at least trying to immunise the populace. But Dr Aslam was unequivocal when she claimed the missile strike would exacerbate the Resurrex problem. It's probably too late to prevent the plague spreading across the whole of the UK.

Three: head to Cheshire and save her father. Her heart aches that she might never again see the old man. Especially since it's her misjudgment that'll likely see him, bewildered and terrified, ripped to pieces bloodthirsty beasts. Is Mr Adderley still alive, though? If he is, would Lena survive the journey to rescue him? Probably not. Even if she did make it as far as the family seat, the likelihood is that the mansion is now home to the undead.

How ironic. The plague I caused could be the only thing that gets dad up and about again. Zombies don't have dementia, do they?

Her fourth option is probably the least viable. She should try to fix the mess she's made, and stop the apocalypse. But how? Aslam, who may have known a way of stopping the crisis, is dead, entombed in the rubble of Evolve HQ. *Along with Harry.* Of all the potential next steps she could take, this is the most hopeless. She wouldn't know where to start. Plus the further into Mortborough she goes, the closer to danger she gets.

Option five, as devised on the roof of Evolve HQ last night, is more realistic. By crafting a narrative blaming eco-terrorists for the Resurrex outbreak, she may be able to minimise reputational damage to the Adderley name…

None of this matters, you idiot! Everyone's either dead, undead or going to die soon. There's no fixing this shit-storm. No one'll care about your stupid family name when this is all over. Not that you can do anything about it, anyway. You're stuck here, Lena, where you belong, with dead people and smashed-up bricks your only company.

Above her, said masonry shifts. The now familiar sound of a minor landslide sets her heart racing. It could be the dead, but she thinks not, for they would move with less caution. The soldiers are a more likely cause, though again, she suspects they would make more noise. They certainly weren't moving stealthily when they were chasing Lena earlier. Nevertheless, she squirms further under the brick-showered table under which she lies. The crackle of nearby gunfire hastens her retreat.

Perhaps it's those children. While her mind's eye has been mostly haunted by memories of rampaging fiends, she has on several occasions wondered about the boy, and the girl whose face she knows. Doing so reminds her of option six. It's perhaps the strangest of her musings and is inspired by a teaching of Islam shared by Aslam shortly before her death.

He who saves a life will be as if he had saved the lives of all humankind.

Of course, the Qu'ran also claims that unjustly killing one person is akin to exterminating all human life, so Lena shudders to think how Allah would judge her part in yesterday's outbreak.

That's done now, Lena. You need to try and put it behind you, and do your best to atone in whatever way you can.

Dwelling on the past, however recent or impactful, won't achieve anything. If, however, she can somehow find those children, and keep them safe, then she *will* be making amends. Not on anywhere as grand a scale as the wrong she's done, but it'll be better than nothing.

At first, imagining the pair of kids only served to further crush her spirits. She contemplated the countless young innocents who've perished so far, plus those who are now orphans, who watched their own parents die and rise again.

Now, though, Lena has a goal. *The boy and girl. I've got to find them. Or try to find them, at least. And if I fail, if I get caught and eaten, or shot by those black-suited bastards, so what? My life's no more precious than any of the thousands that've already been lost, is it?*

So she crawls out from under the old oak table and dusts herself down. Her legs pang when she stands, but after a moment the pain subsides. In the centre of the wreckage-strewn floor, there's a patch of sunlight she's avoided since entering the cellar. Now, falteringly, she steps into the rays and looks up through the hole in the ceiling. She sees a skeletal arm of timber, the remnants of a second storey door frame, perhaps. Then blue sky. The wisp of a cloud. A bird, briefly.

You can do this, Lena. You're not a coward. You fought your way into and out of zombie-central yesterday, and today you've beaten the odds again.

This morning, she dropped into the basement, jarring her knee, but her ascent won't be as painful. A ladder, fully-extended and still half-attached to the fittings that anchored it to the access hatch, lies below the bomb hole. She hauls it upright, positions it under the trapdoor and climbs.

The street outside is visible from the hallway, for the door and at least six feet of the adjoining wall have been blown away, and it appears her way out is clear. Of course, there could be masked snipers watching, but judging by the sound of rifles somewhere close, the men in black have their hands full. Timbers creak around her. A small plane or drone buzzes overhead. Eager to escape the brick dust, Lena steps over chunks of blackened plasterboard and breeze-block.

Out in the open, the sun is warm. Birds twitter to one another, their perches the warped building joists and loft timbers of blitzed houses.

Now, which way?

She vaguely remembers this locale from diversions taken past closed roads in her former life. Taking a left will take her into Mortborough centre; a right turn leads towards the motorway. The children were going towards the former, Lena reckons. With the empty rifle still slung over her shoulder, ignoring the ache in her knee, Lena goes left.

Now she's on a long, straight road that dramatically dips roughly one hundred yards away. The tarmac shimmers in the heat, but she has an excellent view of the road ahead. She sees small figures blundering around; she sees hovering drones; she sees men-in-black. Yet she keeps walking.

I must be mad.

Chapter 39 — Jada Blakowska — 12:50

We're wastin' time. The bikes were facin' away from Mortborough, so that's the way they've gone. It's not rocket science!

Jada tries to catch Brad's eye, but he's preoccupied.

"We've gotta make sure, guys." Not for the first time, Luke's looking unhinged. His hair's a mess, his eyes bloodshot. He's opening wheelie bins, as he did in the other alleyways they checked.

"Luke, bro," Brad says, hands on hips. "We ain't gonna find 'em in no bin —"

"— Thank god you think so too!" Jada says.

The larger of the two men suddenly stops. He smirks, almost starts chuckling, then puffs his cheeks. "Shit, I'm losin' the plot a bit. So which way, then, ya reckon?"

"Back into Mortborough." Brad folds his arms. "They'll be —"

"— What *are* you talkin' about?" Jada explodes. "The bikes were facin' in the *opposite direction*. They obviously saw too many zombies, or soldiers, or drones, and realised tryin' to find their mums was too risky."

Brad looks at his muddy training shoes. "Jus' my opinion."

They're both actin' weird. Luke, 'cause of his son. Brad... "Your opinion makes no sense, though, Brad." *We don't have time for this. Connor needs his dad, an' Evie... I can't let her down, like I did with poor Hanna.* "You wanna go back into Mortborough to settle scores, don't you?"

He looks away. "No. I jus' think —"

"— Woah," Luke interrupts, "would you honestly take us further away from Connor just to try 'n' get revenge?"

"Everythin' doesn't always 'ave t' be 'bout you 'n' Connor —"

"— Never said it did. But what could you ever 'ope to achieve by goin' up against the likes o' Lunt, 'n' those fuckin' drones?"

Brad's head drops. "I don't know. I jus'... I can't keep runnin' away from these pricks. They killed my daughter. I should be goin' after them —"

"— You won't get revenge if you're dead, Brad," Jada says, gently. "The way to beat these bastards is exposin' 'em, not fightin' 'em on the streets."

"She's right. 'N' lettin' Connor die in some crazy attempt to —"

"— Move!" says Brad.

Stone chips erupt from the cobbles underfoot as a cannon roars above. A drone has just flown into view, emerging from behind a derelict mill.

The group scatter. Luke and Brad duck behind a dumpster, pulling its lid open wide to rest against the graffiti'd wall and conceal them from anything above. Jada hides in a doorway. She's out of the UAV's line of sight for the time being, but if it continues on its current flightpath, it'll see her. And rip her to pieces. Hugging the door, she says a silent prayer. Her pulse races; her forehead prickles with sweat. The throbbing in her ankle is forgotten.

The whine of the machine's engine quietens. There's a whirring noise, the shifting of a camera, or gun perhaps. It – or its operator – is assessing the situation. *Probably wonderin' if the three of us are worth the trouble.*

"Move, Jada!" Luke hisses. "If it keeps goin', you'll be dead meat!"

"I know!" She edges forward. Stands on the bottom half of a broken bottle. The crunch elicits another buzz from the drone, then a volley of gunfire. Heart ready to burst, Jada throws herself back against the door. Perhaps the metallic thump, which is directly beneath the UAV, causes confusion, because the hunter/killer becomes immobile once more.

Brad pops his head into view for a second. "Ya need t' make a run fer it!"

Jada shakes her head. "It's too quick," she mouths.

"We'll get its attention. Be ready —"

Again the machine fires, leaving craters in the wall. There's no blood or cry, so Brad must've dodged in time. But the drone's on the move again. Probably attempting to get a better angle on Brad and Luke. *Why doesn't it just fire* through *the bin? It's made o' plastic.*

Now Jada's in the clear. But her two friends are in danger. In just a few seconds, the UAV will espy them, huddled behind the container.

Grimacing, Jada darts forward. She scoops the beer bottle up by its neck and launches it at the aircraft. The glass splinters against its hull; instantly it pivots.

As its camera settles on her, she hears running shoes on cobblestones. Time slows to a crawl. Childhood images flash across her mind's eye; a whimper escapes her throat.

Crack. Something else, a stone maybe, hits the hunter/killer.

"Run!" Luke hollers as, once more, the drone is distracted.

She sprints, passing underneath the robotic predator as she exits the alley.

First it fires to her right, then at her, missing by an inch as she veers to the left, onto a residential street. She spots a half-brick, stoops, grabs, spins. Sees Luke and Brad heading the opposite way. The drone's out above the pavement; it's following the men.

Grunting, she hurls the rock. It misses the UAV but draws its focus, giving the pair the chance to slip into a building. Meanwhile, Jada dashes to the blackened skeleton of a torched van, throws herself prone and rolls beneath the chassis.

She waits. Breathes in through her nose, out through her mouth. Twice the drone fires prolonged barrages, shattering windows, cracking concrete, chewing up wood. Abruptly, its engines whine; at first they get louder, then quickly quieter. *It's going.*

After a minute that feels like an hour, she climbs out from under the van. The UAV is distant now, but she takes the stolen camera from her pocket and snaps a photo. Luke and Brad leave their temporary fort, both wearing haunted grins.

Jada feels the same expression on her own face as she walks to rejoin her friends. "Shit. That was intense."

"Yeah." Luke's still watching the drone, though it shrinks smaller by the second. "Reckon we need t' stay out of the open when we can —" The walkie-talkie buzzes, silencing him. "Josh? 'Ave ya seen 'em, Connor 'n' Evie? Over."

"No, I'm afraid not," Gould's tone is clipped. "But you need to get out of that area. Now. You've got a horde of zombies, about a hundred, heading your way, from central Mortborough. They might miss you, but they might not. Plus another lot, about half as many, coming to meet them from the opposite direction. Over."

Jada sniffs the air: a vile smell is getting stronger.

The trio appraise their surroundings. They're on a short, narrow street featuring four houses, all four of which have been reduced to rubble, and a three storey apartment block that, a couple of smashed windows aside, appears mainly intact.

"We should try 'n' get inside." Jada points at the flats. *'N' hope there's no zombies in there.*

Brad attacks the door with his axe, but to no avail. Using a loose brick from one of the cottages, Luke smashes a ground floor window. They clamber through the opening; Jada gasps as a stray shard of glass draws blood from her right palm.

The undead mob is audible by this point: uneven footsteps, gasps and the rustle of dirty clothes. A flock of birds takes flight in alarm.

It's dark in the corridor, the only illumination the stark neon green of emergency lights.

"Doors all shut." Luke tries one, but the handle won't turn.

"Maybe they'll pass us by?" Brad suggests

Jada looks back out of the window and has to squint at the sun. "Maybe…" The first ragged, bloody figure stumbles into the close. "Maybe not."

Luke and Brad join her to watch the river of dead flesh crashing into view.

"They know we're 'ere," says Brad. Axe swinging, he batters his way through the closest door, which leads to a staircase.

Upwards they go, their steps loud on the steps. Below them, a thud, followed by several more, indicates the zombies have followed them into the building.

"Keep goin'!" Jada says when Luke makes to open the first floor entrance. "To the roof, like we did in the factory!"

"She's right," Brad pants. "It's easier to defend."

"Plus there's scaffoldin' on the back o' the buildin'," Jada adds. "Saw it from the alley. Can use it to get off the roof 'n' back down —"

"— Shit!" Luke's long legs have taken him ahead of the other two. "Stairs are blocked up 'ere. Somethin's come through the window."

Spinning on her heel, Jada aims for the exit onto the first floor. Below, the ground level stairwell door swings open.

Boom.

The explosion from behind the block of flats is alarming, though nowhere near as loud or percussive as those during the missile strikes, last night. Dust motes dance in the light shining through the mezzanine window. A second blast follows, then a third, as they leave the stairway.

"Grenades?" Brad wonders aloud.

"Probably." Jada points to the only source of natural light, at the end of the gloomy corridor they've just joined. "That'll be the back of the buildin', I think. Come on." She starts to run. "If we get outta that window, we can probably reach the scaffold. The zombs'll be too dumb to look outside."

"We 'ope," Luke puffs, matching her stride.

As always, Brad's swiftest. When he reaches the window, he uses the haft of his axe to smash the glass. He's peering outside as the other two catch up.

"Shit," Luke says. "Bit of a climb. You go first, Jada. We'll 'old off the quickest zombs if we 'ave to."

Behind the building there's a fence, and over that, a patch of wasteland littered with dead bodies. While some are prostrate, others shamble across the weeds and gravel. There's movement — *whoever was firing those grenades, probably* — amongst a copse of trees to one side of the clearing.

She needs to focus. The closest scaffold bar, at least a yard away, juts out from the foot platform below by a couple of feet. Undeterred, Jada climbs onto the windowsill and sidesteps onto the outer sill. Gripping the inner window frame with her right hand, she stretches with her left. Her fingers grasp cold metal. *Shit. My grip's not strong enough to take my whole weight in one hand. Need to get* both *hands on it.*

She looks down. Sees hard paving flags. Her stomach roils, but she spots a hole in the brickwork within reach. Without thinking, she prods her left foot towards the indent, digs in her toes and inches along the pipe with her hand.

Better grip now.

More explosions, these closer than before. Ripples of automatic gunfire from the woods behind the fences interspersed with the thrum of bullets hitting meat and wood.

"Hurry," says Brad. "They're on the corridor."

In one smooth movement, Jada pulls herself across to the scaffold pole and grabs it with her second hand. Just as her hold tightens, the cement under her toes crumbles. Dangling, she cries out. She throws her left foot out to the side, kicks wooden board, steadies herself. Then, hand-over-hand, she drags herself onto the scaffold platform.

Axe tucked into his belt, Brad makes lighter work of the manoeuvre. He and Jada haul Luke to safety. The latter's trailing leg narrowly escapes the blackening fingertips of zombie; the fiend leans out of the window and regards the escapees with spite. Suddenly, it topples out, pushed by the pack behind, and hits the ground with a crack.

"Christ." Jada flinches as two more grenades discharge. Assault rifles crackle nearby, plus heavier fire: a light machine gun, probably.

They move along the scaffold. More undead are appearing at the window, and the quickest are attempting to emulate the humans' feat.

Brad chops down the first as it grips the protruding bar.

"No," says Jada. "Cut here." She points at the boards underfoot.

Nodding, Brad smashes the planks into oblivion, while Luke reaches up to unfasten the pole overhead. It comes loose just as another zomb grabs the end closest to the window. The monster's weight drags the horizontal support free; both fall to the floor.

"Up to the next level." Jada indicates a ladder built into the scaffold.

"No! Get down," Brad whispers.

What now? Jada drops to her belly. Dust from the timber boards tickles her nostrils, and Luke's foot is digging into her leg. "What is it?"

"Below us."

She squirms to the left in order to see through a gap between the scaffolding planks. *Nothing there... oh, wait.*

Men in black, carrying rifles, have scaled the fence. They signal to one another but remain silent. Some cover the open window, aiming at the undead still reaching for their escaped lunch. Others, doubtless puzzled by the zombies' desire to exit the building from the first floor, are watching the scaffolding. One finishes the two zombies that have fallen to the ground. "Advance!" he barks; more of the men climb over the fence.

Jada eases the camera from her pocket and captures an image of the paramilitaries, counting fifteen in total.

One of the troops aims his rifle at the window. He fires, but there's no rifle crack. Just a pop followed by a detonation in the building. The scaffolding shakes; Jada holds on to the planks and squints against dust in her eyes. Smoke streams from the hole in the wall. Another grenade is launched, and again the scaffold platform groans and shifts.

"Clear!" the grenadier calls after a moment.

Soldiers go to the two corners of the building, peer around the sides, and give the same assessment.

No, it's not, you dickheads. They're inside *the flats.*

Then the apartment building's windows erupt, spewing forth dozens of zombies.

Chapter 40 — Theo Callaghan — 13:10

Now Gabriela looks angelic again. She has high cheekbones, a dainty nose, tanned skin, rich chocolate-coloured hair. Her warm brown eyes are free of the manic glint Theo saw when she rescued him in the tower block.

She *rescued* me. *As if I wasn't enough of a pussy already, I let a girl save me from the monsters.*

He shakes his head to banish the horrific memory of his near-death experience. And, to his surprise, he *can* forget. Walking through the long yellow grass, in the warm sun, with butterflies in the air, birds in the hedgerows, fresh air in his lungs, beside the most beautiful girl in the world, he can almost pretend the world hasn't ended. If he ignores the frequent crackles of gunfire and occasional explosions in the distance, that is.

They've discussed the last twenty-four hours at some length. Theo's shared his theory of terrorists infiltrating the military, hence last night's bombing and the presence of armed UAVs, though he admitted this premise doesn't explain the rise of the dead. Gabriela reckons some sort of chemical has been released, which is why the inhalers – she has one too – were distributed. She can't explain why they weren't prescribed to everyone, however.

They skirted around the subject of their respective bereavements. The wound is too fresh for Theo; he feared he would become emotional and embarrass himself. Whereas Gabriela told of her mum and dad's deaths in a cool, detached manner.

Maybe she's some kinda psychopath. She saw the zombies eatin' 'er mum. She saw 'em chase 'er dad into the path of a speedin' car, saw 'im lyin' in a pool o' blood, 'ead at a funny angle… but she's alright… all smilin' 'n' shit…

…Don't be ridiculous. People deal wi' grief in different ways…

…But what about the way she looked before, when she smashed that freak's 'ead in… she looked fuckin' mental… badass, though, 'n' cute —

"You're thinkin' about your dad?" she asks sweetly, her accent carrying the merest trace of her parents' Romanian birth.

"Yeah, I guess." He swallows. "You seem… surprisingly okay with it. With, like, yer —"

"Mum an' dad dyin'? I… I'm not. But I'm focussed on Florin now. He is my little brother. When he was born, my mum said it was like *I* was the mother, not she. If I don't protect him… if I can't find him…"

"Me 'n' Evie, we're not *that* close. Not since I went to live wi' Dad, anyway." *I 'ated 'er, t' be honest. Mum 'n' Dad only started to row 'cause of 'er.*

"But she's still your sister, right?"

"Right." *I don't 'ate 'er now. None o' that daft shit matters anymore.* "'N' there's my mum, too. But she could be dead. They both could be dead."

"So could Florin. I just wish he'd never moved school, to Mortborough."

"He was gettin' bullied, yeah?"

"Yes. I kicked their asses twice, but still the little racist bitches carried on picking on him."

They walk in silence for a while. Correctly, they decided that using the fields to travel from Walkley to Mortborough would be safer. It'll take longer, of course, for the land is permanently waterlogged, and their footwear is not appropriate. But it's better to be slow than dead. As they almost were immediately after leaving the Orion complex, when a group of zombies chased them for half a mile.

Gabriela dodges a particularly deep puddle and giggles when Theo fails to do likewise. "You did well before."

"What?" He tries unsuccessfully to shake water from his shoe while hopping. They're going uphill now, and he's getting short of breath. "When?"

"In Great Bear House."

I hid there for hours before I even started lookin' fer ya. "I didn't do anythin', though."

"Yes, you did. You survived."

"Only 'cause o' you."

"I showed up at the last minute. There were tons o' dead zombies there."

"Most of 'em were shot by what's-his-name… Danny…"

"Rowbottom." She scowls. "It's a shame the zombies didn't get *him*."

Theo looks sidelong at his friend. "I know he's supposed t' be a bit of prick, but does he deserve *that*?"

"Definitely. Do you know how he makes his money?"

"Yeah, he's a coke dealer. It's mingin', I know, but —"

"— No, that's not where most of his money comes from. He's a dealer, but he deals *humans* more than drugs. Bastards like him trick people like my mum an' dad, who just want a better life, into comin' over here. Then they have to do horrible jobs, like prostitutes or gang members."

"Fuck 'im, then. But I still feel guilty."

"About what?"

"They were chasin' me when the zombs got 'em. I coulda warned 'em, but I didn't. I just let 'em die."

"Good. 'Cause I heard a girl screamin' before you showed up."

"Me too. Plus, I saw a girl's iPad in one of the rooms, where an ol' bloke 'ad 'is 'ead bashed in."

"Hmm. I think Rowbottom's takin' advantage of all this trouble. Probably kidnapping girls to use as slaves."

"What, like a paedo?"

"Yeah. Or he helps paedos find young girls."

"Ugh. I didn't see any girls with 'im, though."

"Maybe he keeps 'em locked up. Anyway, hurry up!" She turns to face him, having all but reached the summit of the hill they've been climbing.

He's ten yards behind her, sweating in the blazing sun. "Alright, chill out!" Lengthening his stride, he soon catches up; she's stopped, stock still, mouth gape. Now Theo realises why.

Even from a couple of miles away, the ruination of Mortborough is evident. Many of the buildings are smoking, with some aflame. Rows of houses are like a junkie's teeth: some are chipped away to the foundations; others are broken in half; precious few are unaffected. The devastation is not confined to any one area, and a pall of dust and fumes hangs above the whole town. Drones hover here and there. Machine guns chatter. Bigger weapons – *tanks or artillery, maybe?* – belch destruction.

"Like a warzone." Theo shakes his head. "Like something off the news."

Gabriela sighs. "It looks bad. Very bad."

"What are the chances anybody is still alive? The whole place is…fucked."

"We don't know that. It might not be as bad as it looks."

"It might be worse."

They'll all be dead. Mum, Evie, everyone. No one can survive that shit. He thumbs away a tear and sniffs, then remembers Gabriela's next to him.

She puts a hand on his shoulder. "It's okay to cry, you know."

"I'm not cryin'."

"Okay. Let's keep goin'."

"What's the point?" He watches her begin to descend the hill. "Can ya not see what I can see?"

"Yes. Come 'n' walk beside me, and we'll talk."

So he does, and she explains. Her grandmother lived in Bucharest during the Romanian Revolution, when communist dictator Nicolae Ceauşescu violently strove to oppress freedom-fighters. She told many a tale of the chaos and fear that reigned in the winter of 1989.

Though enraptured by Gabriela's natural flare for story-telling, Theo argues that an insurrection, no matter how bloody, could not compare to the carpet-bombing of their destination.

She concedes on this point, but she goes onto relay tales her gran was told by her grandfather – Gab's great-great-grandfather – a Russian immigrant who fought in Stalingrad during World War 2. "This can't be as bad as that, can it?" Looking skywards, she frowns; birds are circling overhead.

"No. I guess not." After climbing over a low stone wall, Theo contemplates the razed suburb once more. He feels like he's in a dream, a nightmare of undead monsters, futuristic flying death-bots and midnight bombing raids. He's walking through dead, knee-high weeds, in the middle of nowhere, without a single scratch on his body. Thousands of his neighbours have died in dozens of ways, yet the Grim Reaper's scythe has missed him every time. "I saw a movie about Stalingrad once, one o' my dad's favourites. About two snipers. One of 'em fell in love, I think. The Russian dude. Not wi' the other sniper, like, with a woman. Anyway, there were survivors. 'N' it looked worse than this."

"We need to keep hopin', keep prayin', and it'll all be okay."

"I ain't prayin' t' no one. Don't believe in all that shit. If there was —"

"— Get down!" She yanks the hem of his shirt.

As he drops to the ground, he feels something brush against him, the passage of an object moving rapidly. A flutter, like a newspaper in a gale. "What the fuck?" Face down, he spits dry grass from his mouth.

Once more, the black thing swoops.

"It's a bird!" Gabriela exclaims.

Theo rolls onto his back. "Birds!" *Shit! Three of 'em.*

Feathers fall, but the crows themselves plunge faster. He raises an arm as one dives. His elbow snags talons aiming at his face. "Arghh! Bastard!"

Gabriela's cursing too. He can't help her, though. Still on his back, eyes slitted against the sun, he has to ward off another of the winged zombies. Flailing fingers catch an eye by pure chance, and the critter shies away. The next time he's ready; he strikes out, punching black avian breast as it descends. Squawking, the bird reels away and lands on its back.

Need t' get up. Make myself a smaller target.

He stands. His friend is still down, hunched over, a raven on her shoulder. She's reaching around the back her own head as if adjusting her ponytail, but she actually has a hold of the creature by one wing. Preventing it from pecking her neck.

Nostrils flared, Theo boots the bird with all his might, tearing it from the girl's back. It hits the ground and flutters its wings one last time. "You okay?"

"Yeah." She straightens up. "Scratched, but alright."

More flapping above: there's one undead corvid left. Theo and Gabriela heft the hammers they stole from 115 Great Bear House. Back-to-back they stand, the rears of their skulls touching as they look to the sky.

"When it drops, move," the girl says.

"Whoever it's closest to, whacks it." The boy licks his lips. Somewhere, nearby, the rotor blades of a helicopter chatter. He doesn't dare avert his eyes from the feathered threat above.

But the crow doesn't attack; it flees.

"It's that helicopter," Gabriela says, pointing.

The black military-style chopper is bearing their way. It's long and bulky yet deceptively-swift. Before long, it's roaring overhead, already low and steadily losing altitude.

"Awesome!" Theo beams. "We're bein' rescued. They can 'elp us find Evie, 'n' mum, 'n' Florin."

"Don't be so sure…"

"What? Why?"

"We don't trust the drones, so why trust helicopters? They could be just as bad. We should hide. Those trees, look, they'll be a good place. They'll make it harder for birds to attack us, too."

The woods are a hundred yards away, down the hill, to the right. As he sprints, Theo's lungs protest, as does his sense of logic. *It's the Army. They can't be hacked like drones, can they?*

Anyway, even if Gabriela's right to be anxious, the naked, starved elms provide poor cover. The children make the best of it, lying on their bellies amidst desiccated vegetation while complaining about their talon-wounds.

The Chinook lands at the base of the rise, approximately two hundred yards from the woods. Its blades cease spinning; for a moment, nothing happens. When the hatches open, Theo's forearms goosefleshes. His bleeding elbow is forgotten. *They're here! The Army'll sort this shit out.*

Except they don't look like British soldiers. They wear all black instead of camouflage, and, worse still, their faces are masked. Theo suspects these men aren't here to help.

Chapter 41 — Floyd Nelson — 13:30

They're making good time. Jogging across fields, they'll be in Mortborough within the hour. *We'll be at da haystack in no time. Ready to search for dat needle by da name o' Lena Adderley.*

Both privates were at the top of their class physically, but in full kit, in thirty degree heat, they're too breathless to talk. Which is a problem. Floyd needs to bounce his thoughts off someone; his mind's a maelstrom of doubt and conviction. So he imagines a conversation between himself and Gurdeep, approximating his squad mate's personality to the best of his ability.

—What ya reckon, den? Dis Lena Adderley.
—Yeah, what about 'er?
—She headin' up dis terrorism ting?
—That's what the man said, innit?

—*Yeah, but… one woman? Causin' all dis shit? Dat seem right to you?*

—*I guess it's pretty crazy. Maybe she ain't workin' on 'er own, like.*

—*Dat'd make more sense, fam. But what about dis 'everyone's a hostile' ting? Dat's bullshit, right dere.*

—*Yeah, probably. Seems a bit… extreme, innit.*

—*Dem youts in da park,* dey *weren't hostiles.*

—*Just kids, bruv. But the brass'll whoop our arses if they find out we didn't smoke 'em.*

—*Don't give a fuck, fam. I's shootin' no youts, ya feel me?*

—*I feel ya.*

—*Reckon dey'll be safe in dat train station?*

—*I 'ope so. Best we could do, innit?*

—*So ya fink dat if we waste dis Adderley gal, we be back wiv da rest o' da boys?*

—*Yeah. That's what that Maguire geezer said, innit?*

—*It'd be cool to be back wiv da boys. None o' dis independent shit. We ain't cut out for special forces, ya get me?*

—*Yeah. But if it means we're forgiven for this mornin', it'll be worth it.*

—*Wonder why they sent us, dough? Two randoms on an important mission. Don't make no sense, bruv.*

—*Maybe we've been genetically-engineered in secret, 'n' we're super-soldiers? The only ones tough enough to beat the zombies, like.*

—*Nah, Gurd. If I was genetically-engineered, dey wouldn't 'ave made me da way I am.*

—What d'ya mean?

—I'm… I like men, not gals.

—That's okay. I do too.

—Is-it?

—Yeah. 'N' I fink… I fink I like you, Floyd—

"Yo, Floyd?" Gurdeep is on his haunches, looking over a low stone wall. "You trippin' or what, bruv?"

"Shit. Sorry fam." Private Nelson shakes his head, drops to one knee and aims his rifle over the stone wall. "Dem trees?"

"No! The helo."

"Shit, yeah. Dey're all wearin' black. We supposed to speak to dem, ya reckon?"

"Don't fink so. Maguire said nuffin 'bout no black ops."

"Don't look like black ops to me. Apart from da uniform. Stood dere, doin' nuttin."

"Hang on. They're movin'. West, same as us."

The Chinook's blades whirr into action, and the chopper lifts off.

Gurdeep checks his PDA and shrugs. "Nuffin on mine. Check yours. See if they've sent that Lisa Adley profile, or whatever her name is."

Floyd checks his own device, but there are no incoming messages. "Nuttin'. Should we buzz Pirie?"

"My comms are down again. Yours?"

Floyd clicks the button on his headset but hears only static. "Same. We'll just 'ave to check again when we get dere."

"We makin' a move, then?"

"Wait." Floyd's eyes narrow. "Da trees. Sometin' dere."

"Fuck that. Unless they come at us, we keep goin', like we done the last coupla times."

"Dem don't look like zombies."

Singh sighs and, like his friend, peers down his rifle scope. "They're small, but that don't mean shit. Ya saw some of the ones in the park."

"I's killin' no —"

"— 'Youts'. Yeah, I know, bruv. I 'eard ya the first thousand times. So we ignore 'em. Keep goin'. Control'll be trackin' us. If we take too long to get to Mortborough, they'll know we wasted time findin' them kids a hidin' place."

Reluctantly, Floyd follows his mate into the next field. He keeps pace as they recommence jogging, but he continues to watch the thicket to his right. *Dem youts, what dey up to?* He slows down to get a better look. *Dey're climbin' da trees! Zombies don't climb trees… unless sometin's up da tree…*

"Floyd!" Gurdeep barks. "Stop fuckin' about 'n' shift yer arse."

There are dogs at the foot of the trees the children are scaling. Floyd uses his gun scope: the animals are rabid, frothing at the mouth, on their hind legs, scratching at the bark. *Zombie dogs, two o' dem.* He drops to one knee, ignoring his friend's complaints, and draws a bead on the larger animal, a German Shepherd. *Shit. What if da black ops guys hear?*

Gurdeep's still remonstrating. "Floyd, for fucksake, just leave 'em be!"

One of the youths must slip, because their foot drops suddenly, to within millimetres of the big canine's jaws. Biting his lip, Floyd squeezes his rifle's trigger. The Alsatian's cranium spurts blood. In a hearbeat he's adjusted his aim and shot the Staffordshire Bull Terrier through the neck.

Using his own telescopic rifle attachment, Gurdeep examines the scene. "Good shootin'. But was it worth the bullets, or the arse-kickin' we'll get for wastin' time?"

"Dere was a kid's foot. Danglin' down from the tree. Dey must've gone 'round da other side of the trunk, or sometin'. Straight up, fam." He begins to run, deaf to Gurdeep's protests.

It's quiet in the grove, as though nature is mourning the two canines' passing. There's a dusty smell, and arid vegetation whispers in the breeze. Stepping carefully, Floyd approaches the tree closest to the German Shepherd's corpse, then angles his path to take him around the trunk. As he does, a limb creaks; a twig snaps. The children are trying to switch to the other side of the tree again, but they're too slow and noisy.

"I can see ya," Floyd says, gently.

Gurdeep arrives, his bearded jaw tense. "You tryin' to get us fucked-up, Nelson? Ya remember what Maguire… oh, shit. Who's that?" He looks up at the boy and girl on their respective branches, his rifle at hip height pointing their way. "Who are *you*?"

"Don't shoot, please," says the girl.

"We won't," Floyd replies. "Come down here."

"Are you British Army?" the boy asks as he struggles to descend.

"Yeah." Floyd gives Gurdeep a glare, but his squadmate lowers his weapon by no more than six inches.

"Those men in black," the girl says as she lands. "Are they with you?"

"No."

Now it's Gurdeep's turn to stare a warning. *Shit, fam, chill. I ain't tellin' dem anytin' compromisin'.*

"Where ya goin'?" Floyd asks.

The youngsters are bloodied and dirty, their faces weary. But there's a defiance in their eyes, too. "Mortborough," the boy declares.

"Why?" Gurdeep's forefinger is now away from his trigger.

"My mum 'n' sister are there."

"My brother, too," adds the girl. "Thanks for shootin' the dogs."

"What ya do to piss 'em off?" asks Gurdeep.

"Nothin'! They're... *infected*."

"We've 'ad birds at us, too." The boy shows angry scratches to his elbow. "They must've been infected too."

Floyd winces. "We goin' Mortborough, too. Ya can come wiv."

Gurdeep frowns. "Walk ten yards ahead of us. No fuckin' about, now."

Thankfully, the teens aren't dawdlers. The two privates can't run, but Floyd's glad of the chance to talk. "See?" He turns to his friend as they splash through a stream fifty yards along the tree line. "Dat 'everyone's a hostile' ting is bullshit."

"Yeah. Fair dues." Gurdeep's watching the sky, seemingly concerned by the kids' tale of predatory crows. "But they must want us to kill this Addersley woman for a reason."

"Yeah. *Someone* started dis zombie shit. But maybe da whole insurrection ting was started in Mortborough, by da terrorists. Dese youts, 'n' everyone else in da surroundin' areas, dey're *not* involved. Just collateral damage, fam. We'll probably find more like dem in Mortborough."

"But not *only* them. Someone caused this disaster, and it makes sense that they're in Mortborough. That's where all the bombs were detonated."

"But why do terrorism in dis shitty little place?" They're emerging from the woods now, with the town in question dead ahead.

The next few minutes are spent recreating the fictional conversation Floyd had earlier with an internal representation of Gurdeep. To the former's delight, it transpires in much the same way as it did in his imagination, though, naturally, he doesn't lead the discussion down the homo-erotic path he took in his own mind. Essentially, while the idealistic Private Singh is more inclined to believe every word from his superiors' mouths, even he has reservations about some of the less credible elements.

Finally, they discuss the implications of escorting the boy and girl. Gurdeep's decided that, as they are masquerading as disaffected army deserters, fraternising with the locals would not seem unusual. Floyd's happy to acquiesce. He also allays his friend's concern that the lad may have been infected by the talon injury to his arm. If, he hypothesises, the zombie plague is spread from one host to another, it'll be by saliva or blood. A peck from a contagious bird could be dangerous, but not a scratch. Probably.

They catch up with the teenagers, who tell their own story. Floyd listens in horror as they describe the deaths of loved ones. Then he and Gurdeep relate a censored version of events since dawn, neglecting to mention the extermination orders and their mission to assassinate Adderley. Instead, they claim they've become frustrated by the Army's preference for locating the perpetrators of the terror attack over addressing the humanitarian crisis. They say they want to help the people affected most severely – those in Mortborough itself.

"There's water up ahead," Gurdeep says, nodding.

"It's a canal," Theo says. "We don't 'ave t' cross it. If we follow it, it leads right into Mortborough. Used to ride m' bike down 'ere."

They pass a black 4x4 near an abandoned farm.

"Q plates," Floyd points out. "Government vehicle."

Gurdeep gives him a funny look but says nothing. They have a choice of two routes. The bridleway will get them into Mortborough quickest, Theo says, but it'll take them away from Florin and Evie's school, so they continue instead down the canal towpath. With a ragged hedgerow on one side, it's secluded enough to make the kids feel safer.

So close are they to Mortborough that Floyd can taste ash and smoke. The acrid stench of burning grows stronger by the minute. The temperature is rising. Smoke and dust drift on a powerful crosswind. There are more drones above now, and the frequent sounds of gunfire is getting louder. "Like we walkin' straight into hell," he says.

The kids, their faces now even grimier, look daunted yet resolute.

"We're not far from the closest houses." Gurdeep points. "Do you two know —"

The roar of an approaching helicopter has them all looking to the east. Like the one that landed near the woods, it's a transport rather than a gunship. And it's descending to land directly in their path.

"Need to find a way past." Floyd looks right and left. The former means crossing the water. The latter is blocked by the hedge; behind that there's a steep ditch, which drops into a disused quarry.

As he prepares to jump into the canal, Gurdeep grabs his shoulder. "Bro. If this is some kinda infection, who knows 'ow it's spread? Could be water-borne."

"I wasn't plannin' on drinkin' it!" Floyd argues.

"Maybe not," Theo says, "but we can't be too careful."

Gurdeep is staring at the water now, a faraway look on his face. At least he's stopped looking at the sky. "There's a bridge, innit, 'bout two hundred metres back. Or we can take that other route."

The group turn back. Floyd's now on the side closest to the ditch, and his right foot hits a rock, sending it through a gap in the hedge and into the quarry. He watches it skip down the gravel; then something else catches his eye just before he walks past the gap. "Shit. Where the fuck did *dey* come from?" He freezes.

There are at least twenty zombies in the ditch, with more scrambling up the quarry side. One catches Floyd's eye. They all look his way, as if governed by a hive mind.

Gurdeep looks over his shoulder. "Shit. We're trapped."

Chapter 42 — Lena Adderley — 13:55

An hour ago she was full of positivity. Recalling the lifestyle coach she dated for a while, years ago, she told herself if she wanted to achieve something badly enough, she could. She visualised the children. She pictured herself dragging them from a burning building. She imagined killing zombies – like the one she shot on the van bonnet this morning, and the one she hammered to eternal death in the DDN depot yesterday – in defence of the innocent.

But reality hits hard and quick.

Although Lena is still determined to help the kids, sheer force of will alone won't be sufficient. Mortborough, or the part she's in at least, is teeming with enemies. All the courage and boldness in the world won't protect her from the men-in-black, drones or mobs of smoke-blackened zombies still wandering the area.

So rather than spending the last sixty minutes searching for the boy and girl, she's been running and hiding for her life. Flitting from bombed building to burnt-out car. And now she's run as far as she can run. Her newfound philanthropy will prove her undoing. *Ironic, really. Being selfish, leaving Harry, almost killed me, but trying to be a good person is what's going to finish me off.*

She was so close, too. As soon as she found the kids bikes, she *knew* where they would be. They'll be hiding in the exact same place she hid once, as a child, when escaping from enemies of a different nature.

Her intuition won't matter now, though, for her luck's run dry. Ten minutes ago, on a high street, she witnessed a dozen zombies slaughtering a squad of black-suits, the first living troops she's seen for a while. She fled. The zombies saw her. They followed.

Thinking herself clever, she went into a local public house well-known for its beer garden on the roof. Because the only time she visited, in her youth, she and her friends noticed that the sun terrace had a neighbour. The townhouse next door had its own roof patio complete with table and chairs. Climbing over the fence separating the properties would be simple. Then she could go down through the private residence, out of the front door, leaving the undead bamboozled.

Except that, like an imbecile, Lena didn't account for bomb damage. The pub and the house appeared unscathed from the outside, especially when compared to the majority of the other properties on Lancaster Road.

Therefore, she finds herself in the open air, on the second floor of The Colliers Arms, with nowhere to go. Slate rubble blocks her path to the townhouse. There's no way of climbing down the side of the building; the safety fence is too high. She's barricaded the door leading back inside as well as she can, but the wicker chairs and foosball table won't last long against ten bloodthirsty zombs. Clearing the debris obstructing the gate to next door, or using the bricks and tiles to strengthen the barrier will take long.

Lena would pour herself a strong drink if almost every bottle behind the bar wasn't shattered by the missile strike. The only liquor remaining is absinthe, which she can't stomach due to a debauched birthday party in Dublin.

Bang bang bang. Like the special forces, the zombies are black, though with soot rather than clothes and masks. She's being chased by death itself; it's pointless to resist. Besides, the kids will be dead soon, if they've not been killed already. She closes her eyes. Maybe she should simply slit her wrists with broken glass, because at least then she won't be reanimated post-mortem. But she's too much of a coward.

An explosion nearby opens her eyes. As if by divine intervention, the first thing she sees is the ruins of the largest of the patio tables. Protruding from under a parasol, there's a nineteenth century-style gas lamp. Miraculously, it wasn't blown up by the air strike. Although its supply of paraffin is all but spent, there might be enough.

Re-energised, Lena grabs the lantern. Then the absinthe. She searches behind the bar and finds a lighter. Using a shard of broken gin bottle, she cuts free a strip of her trouser hem. As she strains to open the lamp, the hammering at the door intensifies. Something falls; glass breaks.

No! I'm not being stopped by something as ridiculous as an over-tightened screw.

She uses her teeth, ignoring the pain as one of the molars chips. A gum bleeds. Then the knob turns, and she sobs with relief.

Bang bang smash. Something's being pushed. Metal scrapes against the concrete floor. They'll be on the short flight of steps leading from door to roof within a minute.

The absinthe's lid loosens more easily once she's wiped her palms dry of sweat. Hands shaking, Lena pours lamp oil into seventy percent strength alcohol. She pokes the polyester trouser strip into the bottle and ties the loose end of material around the bottle neck. Next she uses the dregs from the lantern to prime the wick. Ultimately, she tests the lighter; it works on the third attempt.

Will this work? Such is her only thought as she completes the process. Not once does she have to puzzle over next steps or make a decision; it's almost as though she's prepared a rudimentary firebomb before. Nor is she distracted by the din of zombies trying to breach the blockage she created.

With a final crash, the zombies spill onto the steps below.

Lena lights the Molotov cocktail and throws it down the stairway. The flash is blinding, the heat intense. She has to back away. The result is better than she predicted, given she used no petroleum and only a little paraffin.

They're covered in soot. That's why the zombs are thrashing away, only getting halfway up the stairs before sinking to their knees. After a couple of minutes, the rustle of crawling freaks stops. A small fire burns, which she dowses with a fire extinguisher she finds under the bar. Keeping the extinguisher to use as a weapon, she heads downstairs and out of the pub.

The street outside is clear, so Lena breaks into a jog. Briefly, she wonders at her own ingenuity when incinerating the undead. She's seen movies with petrol bombs, but they're not something she's ever actually thought about. Yet something innate, something almost preternatural, took over. She survived once more. Now those instincts are jangling again, so she checks over her shoulder: nothing.

Two turns later, she enters a lawned area almost clear of buildings. There's only one, a gift shop, and it's dwarfed by the pit head and winding wheel by its side. Mortborough Mine closed forty years ago, a victim of Margaret Thatcher. The museum in its place survived for three and a half decades before a steady fall in revenues took its toll.

At the time, Lena was saddened. She visited the curiosity on seven occasions as a child, enough times to learn from an indulgent, elderly employee about the hidden entrance via the gift shop toilets. Then, as a teen, when she'd all but outgrown the place, her inside knowledge proved advantageous. Hoodlums led by notorious local Danny Rowbotham accosted her while she was jogging. The gang had already been accused of raping one girl, and the daughter of the richest man in town would've been a fine prize.

Young Lena left her tormenters baffled, though. They must've thought she vanished into thin air. After sprinting around the back of the shop, she snuck in through the shop's faulty window, closed it behind herself, prized open the false panel in the women's bathroom closet and climbed down the long ladder to the mine proper. Once sure the boys were gone, she slipped out again. She shared the story with friends; most didn't believe her. Although she never returned to the museum, she always remembered it with fondness. It intrigued her as a pre-teen and kept her safe as an adolescent.

Why does adult Lena think the boy and girl will use the same hideaway? Because of the legend of Mad Morty. Every kid in Mortborough knows the story of convict Mortimer Smith, who was wrongfully-imprisoned for murder in the sixties. He escaped jail, hid in the mine and, thanks to his diminutive size, found a place into which no one else could fit. By the time the authorities completed excavations, he'd disappeared.

However, as she approaches the graffiti-scrawled gift shop, doubts begin to assail Lena. *Kids these days aren't interested in history. They have tablets, phones, VR, all manner of distractions. Worse still, they may not even be from Mortborough. The girl might look familiar, but I could be mistaken. And anyway, even if they do know about Mad Morty, they're unlikely to know about the secret entrance he and I used.*

She's come this far, though. Plus, she was right to trust her gut when she built the firebomb.

Her heart soars when she sees the shop's smashed rear window. *Calm down, Lena. It could be someone else. Or could've been like that for years.* She takes a few deep breaths and squeezes through the opening. She looks at the floor and sees small, black footprints, then realises she's leaving some of her own. It was muddy behind the kiosk. For a moment, she thinks she's heard something else squelching in the mud, but when she pauses, there's only silence.

Wiping sweaty palms on her trousers, she follows the tracks. Into the restroom. The closet's open.

Which is where she finds blood. Only a few drops to begin with, then a larger puddle inside the cupboard.

No, surely not. They can't have come all this way and been caught at the last.

The restroom's lights don't work, so Lena almost misses the bloody fingerprints on the false panel. It appears the kids did make it, after all.

Or someone did, at least. Why am I so convinced it's the two children on the bikes?

The hidden door opens easily; it wasn't closed properly from the other side. As Lena slips through, she hears a bump from the gift shop, and there's no mistaking it this time. She's come too far to go back, however. Hopefully, it's just an inquisitive animal, a cat perhaps.

The descent is long. By the time she reaches the bottom, her sore knee is in agony. Cuts on her hands and fingers have reopened. Upper body muscles ravaged by yesterday's climbing are on fire. She stands still in the dark for a moment, her ears straining, her eyes adjusting to the gloom. A damp musty smell pervades, making her wheeze; Lena takes a hit on her inhaler. Somewhere nearby, there's a light switched on, a torch perhaps. Arms outstretched, she searches for the closest wall.

The light moves. A flurry of movement follows.

Lena's knocked off her feet. Her back and posterior hit hard ground; a scream dies in her throat. Weight on her legs, then chest, something breathing. *Not a zombie.* Cold metal at her throat. "Wait!" she croaks. "I'm not one of them! I'm alive —"

Harsh light blinds her. "Who are you?" a boy asks.

"I'm… I'm..." *The person who started all of this.* "Angelina. Angie." She swallows; the blade nicks her skin. "I'm here to help."

Someone whispers.

"Can you take that knife off me, please? Maybe let me up?"

"Sorry," a girl says.

The torch beam moves, and Lena's eyeballs stop glowing. Squinting, she makes out a brown-haired boy and a blonde girl. "I'm Evie Callaghan," the latter says.

"Connor," says the boy. "Connor Norman. Why ya down 'ere?"

Lena sits up and reaches back to touch chilled stone. "I was looking for you. I saw you riding your bikes, and I thought I'd help you."

"We don't need yer 'elp," Connor replies.

"I can see that. How did you know about this place?"

"M' mum told me about it," says the girl. "She said one of her friends —"

"— Hang on, what's your surname again?"

"Callaghan."

"Your mum… her name's Jennifer, right?"

"Yeah, 'ow do *you* know?"

"She was my friend, at school. I was the one who told her about this hiding place."

"Now yer 'ere," the boy says. "With us. Mental." He goes back to sucking his thumb.

"Are you hurt?"

"I've cut my 'and gettin' smashin' windows open. Twice today."

The blood in the closet. She looks at the wound in the torchlight. "Ooh, that's quite deep." Ignoring the boy's protestations, she tears more material from her trouser hem and bandages the cut. "Listen, I'm not sure how safe it really is down here. We might be better off leaving, if we can."

"It's fine!" the boy replies. "We've got a bit of food. There's no zombies, no drones, no soldiers, no missiles."

"Won't someone be looking for you?"

The boy's head drops.

"He feels bad 'bout runnin' from 'is dad t' look for 'is mum. Thinks 'is dad'll be disappointed."

"He won't care! Honestly, he'll just be glad you're safe." *If he's still alive.* "I take it you've not been able to find your mum?"

"No," Evie says. "Neither of us 'ave. 'N' it was getting' too dangerous. We 'ad t' find somewhere to 'ide. This seemed —"

Directly above them, there's a clang.

Lena gulps. *Shit. I've led the dead down here. I thought I was going to help these kids, and I've done the opposite.*

Chapter 43 — Luke Norman — 14:10

At long last, they're making progress.

An hour ago, from the precarious safety of a scaffold, they watched a horde of undead obliterate a squad of black-clad gunmen. It was a good result for Luke, Jada and Brad.

Shit, I can't believe that's 'ow I'm startin' t' think. People ripped t' fuckin' shreds, 'n' all I can say is "well, it'll be easier t' get away from zombies than bullets." Even so, his cynicism was proven correct. Up onto the roof they went, then back down fire extinguisher at the front of the block of flats. Leaving the host of monsters to scrap over the corpses of the dead paramilitaries on the other side of the building.

By that point, however, the surrounding area was flooded by the dead. They needed forty-five minutes to get back to the kids' abandoned bikes. At least the trip was not in vain, though. Someone, another survivor presumably, started a fire on the top floor of The Colliers Arms pub, and once said person escaped, they headed towards the Mortborough Mining Museum, leaving fresh soot footprints in their wake. At first, their destination confused Luke and his companions, until they realised that the old place would make a good hiding spot.

A call from Gould used the last of their radio's battery, but his brief message was promising. Having spent much of the last hour fighting off undead invaders in the Crawford Centre, he managed, for a short time, to access CCTV footage in their area. The images were poor quality, he said, but they showed two children heading towards the museum.

Behind the gift shop, Luke got the best news he's had all day. Amidst the prints left by the Colliers Arms fire-starter, there are smaller ones. Moreover, the kiosk window is smashed, and Jada's keen eyes find a fibre of clothing attached to a glass splinter. It's the tiniest of strands. But its vivid yellow hue matches the jacket Evie's been wearing.

"Don't get yer 'opes up too much, bro," Brad says as he climbs onto the window ledge.

"Could be a coincidence," Jada agrees. "But if they're not here, we'll still find 'em."

Luke nods, though he can't help the seed of optimism blossoming in his chest.

Brad's about to climb through, when he recoils. "There's zombies in there."

"Shit." Luke switches from hoping Connor's here to the opposite.

"How many?" asks Jada.

"I can see four. No, five."

They probably didn't enter via the window; there would be more blood and broken glass if they had. The group circle the shack and feel stupid when they realise the front door's been breached.

"Right." Brad holds the axe in a two-handed grip.

Luke has a sledgehammer he found on the scaffold. Its weight is comforting. "Ready?"

Jada is the best shot so has the guns. They're virtually empty; the shotgun has the most ammo with only three shells, but it also makes for an effective bludgeon. "You two go in full frontal. I'll arc to the left as much as I can. That way, I'm not firin' over your heads. You two take care o' the quickest to attack, an' I'll make sure the slower ones can't back 'em up."

Good plan. She's a dynamo, Jada,' n' bein' so smart makes her even sexier. If I weren't stressed outta my mind... Luke dismisses the thought and kicks open the damaged front door.

Immediately, a grizzled, bearded zombie lurches towards the entrance. Short and rotund, with eyes for Luke alone, it barrels a postcard carousel aside. Its fingers flex as it jerks towards luncheon, mouth opening and closing like it's already eating.

Teeth gritted, Luke swings the lump hammer. Hard. With a satisfying crack, the ten pound head connects with the beast's chin. Teeth and blood fly; the zomb goes down like a sack of potatoes.

Twice, from the left, Jada's pistol discharges, deafening Luke. Both rounds hit a female monster in the face, sending the slim, burka-wearing figure crashing into a crate of soft drinks left in the middle of the shop floor.

Simultaneously, Brad's axe hits home with a meaty crunch. There's a scraping sound, like a chair leg on a concrete surface. "Shit!" His weapon's blade is stuck in a lanky, tracksuit-wearing male's collarbone. A fourth zombie, a teenaged goth girl with a face full of piercings, is almost on top of him.

So Luke goes to assist, ramming the butt of his hammer into a vampy-lipsticked mouth.

Zombie number five comes from nowhere. Once a little pigtailed girl no more than six years-old, it moves like a monkey. It leaps onto the shop counter. Then jumps and hangs onto a ceiling fan before descending to land on Luke's back. He yells, reaches behind himself.

Again Jada's pistol bangs. Just once this time, but the mini-zomb falls to the ground.

All five enemies are down, twice-dead. "Jesus." Luke experiences an increasingly-familiar yet still-disconcerting sensation: his sensory input lessens – sounds dampen; his vision slows; smells become less distinct – but his ability to think beyond instinctive reactions, to fear, to feel relief returns. *Kinda cool, but kinda weird too.*

They move into the toilets. The men's is empty; dust dances in the sunlight streaming through the frosted window. However, the linoleum floor of the ladies' room has muddy footprints of various sizes and treads, which lead to a closet. Blood's on the lino and around the edges of a board in the wall. Brad readies his axe, but Luke prises the panel open with his fingers.

"It's dark." Jada peers into the void. "Deep, too."

"'Ow can ya tell that?" asks Luke.

"Dunno… just a feeling I get."

"That ladder is a pretty good clue, too," says Brad, deadpan.

"Oh, yeah."

Five minutes later, they're at the bottom of the shaft. In total silence. The darkness is almost as absolute, but there's light somewhere down the narrow corridor in which they find themselves. Everything is muted apart from the odour, which is that of a tomb. Infected by the oppressive silence, the group head towards the source of illumination.

At first, it seems the light is getting no closer. As if it too is moving, but away from them. Soon they hear movement, then voices. Luke's at the front, so he's the one to walk into a wall. "Stop, guys." Grimacing, he rubs his knee and turns right.

The rock flies a centimetre wide of his face to splinter against the wall behind him. Meanwhile, bright torchlight blinds him. "Stop!" He shields his eyes. "I'm not one o' *them*!"

Then he feels arms around his chest. A head nuzzling into his breastbone.

"I'm sorry, Dad," Connor says, his words thick with emotion.

Luke ruffles his son's hair. "Ya little bugger." A warm eruption surges from his heart to his extremities; it's an elation he can't describe. *I'm never lettin' 'im go again.* He squints over the boy's shoulder and sees Evie, plus a woman shrouded in shadow, holding a fire extinguisher and a torch. "Who are *you*?"

The flashlight is lowered: now Luke can make out the stranger. She's roughly thirty years of age, though it's still too gloomy to see her features.

"My name's Angie. Angie Acton." She comes a little closer to the bend in the tunnel. While happy to acknowledge him and Brad, she seems more wary of Jada, who's making a fuss of Evie. "I used to work here, at the museum." She looks furtive. Perhaps it's just the darkness, but she seems unwilling to come too close.

Luke takes his son under the chin, gently, and raises his face. "What were ya thinkin'?"

"I just…" Connor's voice is brittle. "I —"

"— We needed t' see fer ourselves." Evie's a few inches shorter than her friend, but she has more confidence. "Everyone kept sayin' our mums were dead. But 'ow could ya know fer sure?"

"We couldn't," Luke admits, he looks at Jada, but she's still focussed on the newcomer, Lisa.

"I shoulda listened t' ya." Luke sighs. "I'm sorry." *I'm probably gonna regret this, but if I ignore what Connor wants again, I could lose 'im again.* "Is there are anywhere else ya wanna look, when we're out of 'ere?"

"I don't think there's much chance o' findin' Mum," the boy answers, his lip quivering, "but Evie's brother 'n' dad live in Walkley…"

"Okay, well, we need t' go back there anyway, so I suppose we can check it out —"

"— Guys." Brad's backed away and is a few yards behind them. "Sorry t' interrupt, but did no one else 'ear that?

"What?" asks Jada.

"Shh, 'n' you'll 'ear."

Everyone falls silent. Sure enough, there's a banging sound coming from the shaft they've just descended. The two children look ready to cry.

"Is there another way out?" Jada asks.

"There'll be a main shaft, right?" Brad begins to creep towards the secret exit. "What the miners used t' come down."

"It was all blocked up, years ago." Angie Acton isn't moving.

"Connor, Evie, stay with Jada." Luke, feeling his way along the corridor, catches up with Brad. "Maybe we can fight our way out this way," he whispers. Before long, he sees a patch which is fractionally-less dark than his surroundings. He can just about make out the base of the ladder. Another bump sets his heart pounding, and falling dust makes him cough. He stifles the splutter with the back of his hand.

"Me first?" Brad tucks his axe into his belt and puts one hand on the ladder.

A smash above causes another shower of dirt. More light. A frantic rustling.

"Move!" Luke grabs his friend by his hood and hauls him backwards.

A body lands at their feet with a loud slap. Like a wet rag thrown into a window. Warm wetness sprays in all directions, coating Luke's feet and shins. The two men raise their weapons, but the face-down zombie isn't moving. It's silent, but it reeks.

Gingerly, Luke grabs the former woman's ponytail and yanks her head back. The illumination from above remains meagre, but the ruin of the creature's face is chastening still. Black coal residue adheres to a red, sludgy, flattened mess. "Jesus."

"Just threw itself down." Brad shakes his head. "Come on, let's get back —"

Another impact, another lemming-like zomb, this one landing on the first's back. Blood erupts from both.

Then a third; another fine liquid mist squirts.

The fourth hits as Luke and Brad stop gaping and turn tail to run.

"We need to find another way out," the former says when they rejoin the others. He explains the situation at the foot of the ladder; regular thuds echoing down the corridor bear testimony to his summary. As he speaks, he senses tension between the two women. Jada's holding the torch now.

"If they're just gonna kill 'emselves, why the rush?" Brad wonders.

"Because eventually," Angie begins, facing away from everyone, "if there's enough of them, they won't fall far enough to die. There'll be a pile, and the jumpers will land on the pile…"

"Gross," says Evie; Connor sniggers.

"I think there might be another way…" Again, Angie's voice trails off; it doesn't help that she's keeping her distance and looking in the opposite direction.

"*Angie*," Jada interjects. "We can't really hear you. Why don't you come closer?"

"I'm photo-sensitive," the other lady replies, "and you keep shining that bloody torch in my face."

"That's because I want to see you properly."

"Jada, why ya bein' weird?" Brad asks.

"I don't think Angie Acton is really called Angie Acton."

"Eh?" Luke flinches at a particularly loud smack from down the passageway.

"I think her real name is —"

"— Lena Adderley. My name is Lena Adderley," the other woman says, almost proudly. "I'm sorry for lying to you."

"— So what?" Brad shrugs. "Who gives a shit? Bit strange ya gave us a fake name, but…" Catching Jada's eye silences him.

Arms folded, the journalist is glowering at Lena.

Lena Adderley. That's the Evolve boss Jada suspects. Responsible for this whole fuckin' thing.

"Your company," Jada says, "Evolve, you caused all this shit, didn't you?"

Briefly, the older female has her hands on hips, ready to defend herself. Then she deflates – audibly, with a cross between a shudder and a sob. "Yes, it was my company that caused the outbreak. It wasn't something we could ever prepare for, not something we could ever foresee. We took all the precautions we could —"

"— Bullshit!" Jada explodes. "You had a dissentin' scientist, Dr Sofia Aslam. I was gonna interview her. She warned you —"

"Ha! Aslam left the company *three years ago*! In fact, we weren't even called Evolve then! She's a crackpot with a list of mental illnesses as long as your arm."

"So you say. We'll never know now, probably. Those missiles have destroyed any evidence."

"Maybe. But I'll happily admit my part, my company's part in all this. I promise you that if we survive, I will hand myself into the authorities."

"I'll hold you to that."

"I'll hold *myself* to that. I'm not evil, Jada. Nor were my employees. We were trying to save the world. Everyone knows how desperate things are getting. But unlike most, we had a solution."

"A solution that failed. An' destroyed our town!"

"I know." Lena's head drops. "It's my town, too."

She's gonna 'ave that on her conscience till the day she dies. 'N' yeah, her company were tryin' t' make things better fer everyone. They messed up, badly, but the world's probably fucked anyway. He looks at Jada.

She still eyeballs her adversary, but she's lost some of her steam. "So you'll corroborate my story? You'll own up to what your company's done?"

"I will. You can interview me in jail, if necessary."

She's got some balls. Fair play to 'er.

"An' what about anyone else involved? The Government."

"I'll tell the truth. Fuck the Government. They'll —"

Brad's roar and tackle takes everyone by surprise. In a blink of an eye, he has Lena on her back with his hands at her throat.

Chapter 44 — Jada Blakowska — 14:40

She's the quickest to react. While Luke's still standing, agape, Jada's on Brad's back, her forearm around his throat, her fingers laced. Pulling back with all her might.

He's weakening. Almost sobbing, such is his anger. "Fuckin' bitch, fuckin' bitch, fuckin' bitch..." His voice becomes a wheeze, yet still he won't stop strangling.

On the ground, Lena's squealing in pain and panic.

And finally, after a few seconds that feel like hours, Luke acts. He's far bigger than Brad. Even so, he struggles to prise his friend's hands from the businesswoman's throat. Eventually, the pressure from Jada's sleeper hold takes a toll, and Brad relinquishes his grip.

Lena weeps, whimpers, and splutters, but she does not protest. Nor does she move. *She knows she had it comin'.*

Brad is on his knees by her side, head in hands. Still he repeats the mantra: "Fuckin' bitch, fuckin' bitch."

Luke, with an arm around Connor, is attempting to calm himself.

Jada has a hand on Evie's shoulder; she's telling the kids that everything will be alright.

Both children are silent, their faces blank, eyes dry.

"You killed them." Brad's voice is low now, almost conversational. "You killed *her*. My little girl LaRosa. Why should you live?"

"I'm sorry," Lena rasps. "Truly I am."

Meanwhile, approximately every ten seconds, there's a splatting noise from the far end of the passage. The sound is changing; it's become more muffled, less violent.

"Sorry don't cut it," Brad insists. "I'm gonna kill you, Lena Adderley. I fuckin' swear down —"

Luke clears his throat. "Kids, what was she doin' with you two?"

"Whaddya mean?" Connor turns to face his father.

"Why was she 'ere?"

"She wanted t' look after us, she said," Evie squeaks.

"Said somethin' 'bout makin' a men."

"Making amends," Lena states. "I wanted to protect them, to atone for all the deaths I've caused."

"It'll take *a lot* more than that." Brad is up on his feet again. A black energy pulses from his body, from his very soul. "But we'll call it even when I cut yer fuckin' 'ead off."

Shaking his head, Luke moves to intercept his friend, but Jada holds her hand aloft.

"Brad," she starts, "killin' Lena won't give you justice. 'Cause she's not the only one to blame. Evolve should've taken more care. *Far* more care. But it's not *their* job to protect us. It's the Government's. They should've stopped this happenin', an' they enabled it instead. They *sponsored* it."

"So?" Brad turns a baleful gaze on her. "The Government aren't 'ere. We can't do shit 'bout them, can we? But we can punish *her*. We can —"

"— Jesus, Brad!" *Why is everyone else so dumb?* "Think for a goddamn minute. We can use Lena to nail the Government. They're the real culprits here. An' they're the ones sendin' special forces, an' drones. They've nearly killed us twice today."

Brad makes no reply. His breathing is surreally-loud, and it's the only sound apart from the regular drip-drip of zombies landing at the base of the ladder.

"I was wrong, Brad." Lena's voice is raw. "I'm sorry to all of you. Evolve should've done more trials. We shouldn't have bowed to Government pressure."

"I thought ya said ya took *all* necessary precautions," Luke observes.

"We did, but we should've made triple sure. I was corporate, never involved with the practical side, but I should've done more. And I'll admit, when all this started yesterday, I didn't react in the right way. I don't think it would've made any difference to locals like you three, but I was too focussed on following Government orders. And... and —"

"— An' what?" demands Jada.

"Protecting my family's reputation."

"Your *family's reputation*?" Brad spits.

"Yes." She tells of her father's dementia, and even Brad softens a touch towards her. "Believe me, I want to get back at the Government, too." She relates the final conversation she had with Gordon Villeneuve MP yesterday, when it became clear he was prepared to obliterate a whole town to insulate himself and his employers against culpability. "I want them to pay for destroying Mortborough. I know I need to pay as well, and I'm willing to take my medicine, but we created Resurrex for the right reasons. There's no justification for what Villeneuve decided to do, though. The missile strike. No justification for what he's continuing to do, sending troops and drones to kill survivors and zombies indiscriminately."

When she finishes speaking, everyone is quiet for a moment.

I thought the missiles, troops an' drones were an overzealous attempt to contain the threat. I didn't truly believe the Government's first priority was savin' their own skins.

"Anyway," Lena says as yet another thump signifies the fall of a zombie, "we still need to get out of here. If you want to carry on arguing about this, if you still feel you need to take revenge against me personally *after* we're out, fair enough. But let's do that when we're not within a few yards of a growing pile of the walking dead."

She's right. An' she's used to bein' in charge. She has a natural authority. "You got anythin' in mind?"

"Yes. There is a third exit. The old railroad the mine used to ship its coal out."

"Where?" says Luke, taking Connor's hand.

Lena takes the flashlight from Jada. "This way." She strides down the corridor, heading away from the ladder.

They're setting off when there's a different sound behind them: like a rockslide if the boulders were bales of hay. Then footsteps. The dry smell of coal and earth is being overpowered by that of rotting bodies.

"Run!" Jada yells.

Connor and Evie jump on Luke and Brad's backs respectively, which means the two women are fastest. Her gaze intent on the bouncing beam of torchlight, Jada follows Lena. In parts, the floor is treacherous. She slips on wet stones, skids on small dry ones, nearly stumbles over larger ones. By the time they turn the first corner, going right, she's blowing hard. She risks a glance over her shoulder. The two males, lagging behind, are barely visible in the darkness.

All is silent, apart from their footfalls and the bustle of the chasing pack.

"Is it far?" Jada pants.

"A minute, maybe two?" Lena's ten paces ahead and barely out of breath. She slows and points the torch over her shoulder.

Luke and Brad, laden with children. Behind them but gaining ground, a stream of ugly undead faces. The men turn, see the horrific procession and redouble their efforts.

A left turn leads to a gate, which, mercifully, is closed but not locked. Through the portal they go – an iron clank to their rear suggests Luke or Brad has barred it behind them – then another left.

"Watch the rails!" Lena calls, angling her torch-beam downwards just in time to stop Jada tripping.

They follow the mine cart tracks down a subway at least thrice the breadth of the previous one. Jada's lungs scream for respite; she feels like she's running through treacle rather than on gravel. All she can do is focus on the torch's paltry illumination. Until she sees another source of light, up ahead and to the right. The end of the tunnel beckons.

"Nearly there!" Lena sounds exerted for the first time.

A metallic jangling in their wake probably means the zombs are through the gate. Sure enough, the rustling noise and the stumbling staccato of dead footsteps recommence. Quieter now, further away. Yet the noise swiftly increases in volume; the undead have fallen behind, but the greater width of the railway tunnel means they're accelerating, gaining ground.

Just keep goin'. Daylight's in sight.

But it's being obscured. Three dark shapes are appearing, blotting out the sunshine. She unslings the shotgun from her back; it has three rounds left. She needs to make them count.

Chapter 45 — Theo Callaghan — 14:50

He's still shivering, but he's not allowed to stand at the window and dry himself in the sun. They might be spotted. In the wasteland to the north, there are now at least fifty heavily-armed troops. With more being airlifted in by helicopters on a frequent basis, plus a tank. *A big fuckin' tank!*

To escape the quarry undead, they had to wade across the canal. Their foes were flummoxed by the water, for a while at least. By the time the first zombie braved the swim, Theo, Gabriela, Floyd and Gurdeep were already scrambling onto the opposite towpath. A damp-smelling timber boathouse thirty yards downstream provided the perfect hiding place.

Through the second storey window, the unlikely foursome watched the zombs cross the waterway. When they emerged from the murky flow, they were like sniffer dogs thrown off a scent. They meandered about on the canalside, aimless, before eventually heading in the opposite direction to the boathouse. Though separated by no more than a line of trees, a road and a hundred yards, the half-century of troops and the monsters were unaware of each other. Just as they were oblivious to the two servicemen and the pair of local kids hiding nearby.

Despite himself, Theo is enthralled. Meeting two real soldiers, Floyd and Gurdeep, was impressive enough, and now he's a stone's throw from four dozen more. *And a massive tank!* The small army don't wear HM Forces uniform, but he feels a swell of national pride nonetheless. *These guys will get shit done. The zombies don't stand a chance.*

"What are you smilin' about, Theo?" Gabriela's not at the window; military manoeuvres are of no interest to her.

"Nothin'. Just… I think everything's gonna be okay now. The Army are startin' t' take this really serious. 'Boots on the ground', they usually call it. Whenever they start sendin' actual men in, that's when they're really gettin' into it." *That's 'ow it is in the movies, anyway.*

"Come away from that window," Gurdeep warns.

Theo obeys with a frown. "What's so bad about 'em seein' us, though? They can come 'n' —"

"— We don't be assumin' nuttin wiv dese guys," Floyd says. He's tall, lithe and muscular, with the natural authority of an older man. "Dey not British Army, fam. Dey're not 'ere to save da day. Dey'll shoot us on sight —"

"— Ya don't know that, dickhead." Gurdeep shakes his head in exasperation. "*You're* assumin' shit now."

"What do *you* think, Gabriela?" Theo asks.

"Hmm. I don't know." She screws up one eye, which makes her look even more adorable than usual. "The black uniforms scare me. I don't know what it is about them. Just makes me think they're bein' sneaky."

"Yer gal's makin' nuff sense, Theo." Floyd begins to pace again, while keeping clear of the window. "I don't trust dem one bit." He looks at Gurdeep. "You a fool for finkin' dey kosher, bruv."

"I'm not fuckin' sayin' they're kosher, am I? *I'm* the one who keeps tellin' peeps to keep outta sight. Bottom line, I'm not sure. Ain't sayin' we can defo trust 'em, but I ain't sayin' they're out to get us, either. The only ones who I know will kill us are those ugly, stinking zombie fucks."

There's somethin' they ain't tellin' us. Why wouldn't they trust other soldiers? Theo risks another glimpse out of the window. The tightly-packed mass of black-suited men is stationery, bristling with rifles. *They don't look like they're in any rush to start kickin' arse 'n' savin' lives.* "Why aren't they doin' anythin'?"

Floyd and Gurdeep shrug.

"Why don't ya just go 'n' speak to 'em?"

Floyd and Gurdeep exchange a loaded glance.

"We need to trust each other, if we're gonna stick together," Gabriela states.

"Maybe we won't stick together, then," Gurdeep replies, his eyes cold.

Floyd flashes him a look of annoyance. "Ignore 'im. You're wiv us as long as ya want." He again turns to his friend, but this time his gaze lingers on the side of Gurdeep's hairy face. "She got a point, bruv."

For a moment, Theo forgets the zombies and gunmen outside, his missing family, the crisis enveloping his hometown. *I could be accepted by them. That'd make me, like, their brother-in-arms, or somethin'. I might even get a gun —*

Gurdeep's nostrils flare. "Word outside, Private Nelson."

Floyd rolls his eyes. "Can't go outside, Private Singh. Dere's zombies 'n' special forces 'n' shit out dere."

So the pair walk across the boathouse floor, skirting the motorboat by the double doors leading to the water. Meanwhile, the two teenagers unfold a couple of camping chairs and take a seat, Theo grimacing as his saturated trousers squelch under his bottom. The Sikh leans in to whisper something in the Afro-Caribbean's ear; the latter replies in the same manner. Their mutterings quickly escalate to hisses, followed by low growls accompanied by pointing index fingers. Briefly, it almost seems physical violence will ensue, but then they return to the kids.

"Okay," Floyd says. "I fink yer both right. Gurdeep agrees wiv me now —"

"— Don't *fully* agree wiv ya," Gurdeep interrupts.

"Whatever. Listen. Da reason dem soldiers are still stood dere, doin' nuttin, is this."

Theo and Gabriela wait.

"Well, it's just dat… dey… put it dis way. Dis ain't no humanitarian mission."

Gurdeep is fidgeting as he watches his comrade speak, as though anxious he'll divulge too much information.

"Peeps like you ain't da priority," Floyd continues. "I know dat —"

"— So what is the priority, then?" asks Gabriela, her lip curled.

"Dealin' wiv the zombies," Gurdeep states.

There's silence for a moment, during which Theo begins to slowly shake his head. *Don't make no sense.* "I don't believe you."

Floyd winces, and Gurdeep puffs his chest, but neither responds.

Gabriela turns to face her friend. "What don't you believe?"

"Forget the black uniforms. Maybe that's just somethin' to confuse the zombs… I don't know. But they're the British Army. *Our* army. They'll protect us, just like they would if there was a proper war, 'n' another country was invadin' us. That's their job, innit? To protect England, the UK or Britain or whatever." He shakes his head again, more vigorously this time. "They're the *good guys*."

Although Gabriela smiles, it's not an expression Theo appreciates. She's regarding her schoolmate with pity, affectionate pity maybe, but condescending all the same. "Things aren't so black and white." She's trying to speak to him like an equal. "I don't blame you for feelin' this way, though, because your beliefs are part of who you are."

I don't get it. She's only a few months older than me, so why's she so much more mature? "What're ya sayin'?"

"Okay, let me try to explain. You're patriotic, right?"

"Yeah."

"You like soldiers. You like planes, helicopters, missiles, all that stuff?"

"Well, maybe not missiles after last night, but yeah. Why?"

"Why do you like all those things?"

"I dunno."

"Movies? Video games?"

"Well, yeah." He raises his eyebrows. "Books too. I'm not a dumb-ass, ya know."

Her face opens: she's impressed. "There's more to you than meets the eye, Theo Callaghan. But that's all fiction, right?"

"Not all of it. But yeah, most of it. So?"

"Remember I was tellin' you about my grandmother, an' her grandmother, in Romania?"

"Yeah?"

"The army weren't the good guys then. They weren't the good guys in any o' the other communist countries either."

"Yeah, but that was the Cold War, right? The Russians were the bad guys."

"Okay, but the Americans did bad stuff as well. Read up on Vietnam, and Nicaragua."

"Nicar-where?"

"It's in South America."

Theo frowns, shifts in his chair.

Gurdeep's attention is wandering. He's gazing out of the canal-facing window; in fact, he's moving to get a better look, but Floyd seems intrigued by the conversation.

"What's this gotta do wi' the zombie apocalypse in Mortborough, though, Gabriela?" Theo asks.

"There's no good guys or bad guys," Floyd says with conviction.

"Exactly!" Gabriela grins.

She really is beautiful, 'n' smart. Way outta my league ."So we don't trust the Army. But what then?"

"We go our own way. We trust people *like us*."

"But not like Danny Rowbotham."

"No, not like him."

"They've gotta do somethin' sooner or later, though, right? The soldiers in black, like."

Floyd nods. "Dey ain't flyin' 'em in for da fun of it. So we wait for dem to move." His eyes flicker towards Gurdeep, and his voice lowers. "Den we carry on into town. Find yer family. Get da fuck outta dere."

If Private Singh realises plans are being made without his consent, he doesn't show it. He's fixated on the view of the water, or rather the path running alongside.

After winking at the children, Floyd joins his squadmate at the far end of the boathouse. They talk quietly.

Gurdeep's demeanour is tense, his fists balled.

Soon Floyd shares his bearing. He returns to his wards and, with a sigh, signals for them to rise. "Right. We need to make a move."

"What's up?" Gabriela wonders.

"Dem zombies dat crossed the river —"

"— Canal," insists Theo.

'Whatever. We thought dey be goin da other way. Dey did, at first. But now dey've turned 'round."

Keeping low, Theo goes to see for himself. The watercourse sparkles in the sun, so he has to squint. All he can see, in the distance, are a few forms on the footpath.

"'Ere, use this." Gurdeep hands the boy his rifle so he can use its scope.

Hands trembling – *I'm 'oldin' an actual, loaded, British Army issue SA80* – he raises the lens to his eye. "Thanks." The indistinct figures become walking dead people, splattered with blood and dirty water. "Shit. There's, what? Thirty of 'em?"

"Double that. Can't you see the ones in the water?"

"Shit, yeah."

"So we snipe fuck outta dem." Using the butt of his gun, Floyd smashes the pane of glass. "We killed this many before —"

"'Cept we can't be firin' 'ere," Gurdeep argues. "The men-in-black are still over there. They'll 'ear us. We can't carry on down the towpath, 'cause that'll take us straight past 'em."

"Maybe we can go back over the water," Gabriela suggests. "Into the quarry."

"Dat's where dey was comin' from originally, dough." Floyd's stopped looking out of the window and is appraising the motorboat instead.

"You finkin' what I'm finkin'?" Gurdeep asks, slapping the boat's hull.

"No clue 'ow to drive one o' dese, dough. You?"

"Ya don't drive a boat, dickhead. Ya *sail* it —"

"We can do it," says Theo. "Right, Gabriela?"

"Right." She smiles, hold his gaze for a moment.

School trip last summer. The Lake District, boating on Windermere. Happiest hour o' m' life so far. Just me, Gabriela, two other pupils, 'n' the boat guy.

Gurdeep slings his rifle over his shoulder. "So if we get it on the water, you two can dr— I mean, sail the boat?"

"Reckon so." Theo turns back to the canal-facing window. The dead are getting closer, their features now distinguishable with the naked eye. "Let's get it in the water, quick."

Gurdeep uses the butt of his rifle to smash the old padlock on the double doors giving access to the water. Floyd and the kids work on untying the vessel from its stand.

By the time the boat's being rolled into the water, its trolley wheels squealing, the fastest of the undead appear at the window. Theo takes one final glance out of the opposite side: the black-suits have registered the nearby horde. Some are deploying to investigate. The sound of the outboard motor is sure to further pique their interest, but it can't be helped.

The engine starts second time. In truth, Theo and Gabriela's 'specialist' knowledge is barely required. Either of their siblings could figure it out. The sound of breaking glass and footsteps on floorboards in the boathouse only serves to sharpen their minds. With Gurdeep at the helm, the watercraft begins to move just as the first zombie splashes into the canal. It dives to grab hold but, thanks to the propeller, loses its hand in the process. The brown water is tainted red as the hapless freak paddles.

"Fank fuck for dat!" Private Nelson's still aiming his gun at the ghouls in their wake.

Thank fuck fer that indeed. Now, we should get to —

A knock to the starboard side of the boat causes Floyd to wobble.

Shit. The zombies in the water. They've waded straight past the boathouse...

A wet hand, one of its fingers a bloody stump, grips the rim of the craft. Another one, this one gloved and more dainty, appears on the port side. Floyd regains his composure and raises his rifle. He fires as soon as a bald, scarred head pops into view; the high velocity round, at almost point blank range, sprays skull, brain and blood as far as the closest bank. The private's second shot produces almost identical results, except this time it's a bleached blond ponytail bobbing on the water amidst the grey matter and bone fragments.

Aqua-zombie number three is slain while it's still in the water. Three single shots, all economical kills, the reports sickeningly-loud in the open air.

"Ya didn't have to shoot 'em, bruv," Gurdeep complains. "Coulda just whacked 'em away, or somefin'. Those soldiers catch us, we're fucked. Shot as deserters."

Floyd doesn't reply. He acted in panic, and his face betrays his regret.

The motorboat accelerates as Gurdeep opens the throttle. Its hum can't drown out a new noise, though: a creaking, rolling sound, one Theo knows from films and console games. *The tank's comin'.*

Chapter 46 — Floyd Nelson — 15:15

Dis boat is too slow!

The tank's getting louder. Soon enough, it'll plough through the hedge running the length of the towpath. And it'll blow them out of the water like a bear swiping a salmon.

"Why ain't it speedin' up?" asks Gurdeep.

"Top speed?" suggests Theo. "It's not a speedboat."

"Well, we need to fink of a way to beat a tank. Any ideas?"

The boy blinks. "I'd never even seen a tank in the flesh till twenty minutes ago!"

"Wait a minute." Gabriela's watching the bank closest to the wasteland. A duck is on the edge, watching the approaching boat with beady eyes.

Theo has begun to pace the deck. "This is no time for bird-watching, Gabriela. We need —"

"Shut up! Look at its feet."

"What?" Floyd, Gurdeep and Theo say in unison.

"Ah," the latter says, pointing.

The clay at the edge of the bank is crumbling, coming away in chunks, just from the weight of the fowl.

With a crunch of twigs, the armoured vehicle materialises. Thirty yards behind the boat, it gains speed, driving parallel with the canal. Half on the towpath, half crushing the hedgerow. Its cannon is turning their way.

"Slow down," says Floyd, ignoring the nausea induced by the big gun and its wide, black muzzle. *Gonna take dis motherfucker down a peg or two.* "I got a plan. Gurdeep, stop the boat. Kids, copy me." He raises his hands in surrender.

The two teens do likewise.

"Gurd. C4. Quietly. On the bank, next to the bastard. Then dust."

"I've barely got enough to blow a door, Floyd! You know that!"

"Just do it, fam."

As the vessel comes to a stop, so does the tank. Gurdeep's fumbling with plastic explosives, using the steering wheel to hide his efforts.

Come on. Hurry up, fam!

Suddenly, the package is airborne. A split-second after landing beneath the tank's tracks, the C4 detonates. The ground beneath the big metal beast shifts. Crumbles. The front left quarter of the vehicle drops, pulling the remainder with it into the water, submerging the cannon. The ensuing wave pushes the boat forwards. Gurdeep cranks up the throttle. And they're away.

Perhaps the barrel of the tank's cannon has pierced the canal bed, because the tank is anchored at a tilt, its rear at a forty-five degree angle to the water. An officer in black emerges from the turret. Briefly, he's confused by his orientation. Then he levels his rifle.

"Get down!" Floyd flattens himself against the deck. Wood splinters; passing bullets whine; the windshield glass shatters.

Now they're away. Troops appear on the towpath, but they're too far away, too slow to pose a threat.

Floyd takes a deep breath. He tastes smoke in the air, smells the coppery-undertone of the canal water. While the kids sit down, shell-shocked, he joins his fellow private at the wheel.

"What the fuck 'ave we done?" Gurdeep's talking in a low voice, licking stray strands of his moustache. "We've fired on our own side, Floyd. Our *own, fuckin', side.*"

Floyd sighs. "What choice did we 'ave, bruv? Dem black-suits don't know 'bout dis mission from Maguire, do dey? Dey'd have treated us like deserters —"

"Ya don't know that! Maybe they was gonna wave us on our way."

"Doubtful, bruv. 'Specially not wiv da kids on board."

"We'll never know now, will we? But either way, the Adderley mission was supposed to be confidential. Sinkin' a whole fuckin' tank wasn't part o' the deal."

They travel in silence for a minute. A bend to the right gives them a better view of Mortborough, with its columns of fumes and drone-infested skies.

"End o' the line." Gurdeep points: fifty yards up ahead, there's a lock, and it's closed.

"Time to get out," Floyd tells the children; they nod dumbly.

Once the boat has stopped they alight. The reek of fire is stronger than ever, but it's better than that of decomposing bodies. Soon, they reach the first housing estate and a petrol station. All is destroyed. Even this far from the town centre, nine out of ten buildings are razed. Realising the futility of their search, Theo and Gabriela become visibly distraught.

"Ya never know," Floyd says, circumnavigating the wreckage of a bus. "There could still be people alive, somewhere."

The youngsters don't answer. They don't have to; the reality of the smoking hell around them says more than a thousand words. Tuesday's not as warm as Monday, but Mortborough radiates its own warmth. Sweat pours down Floyd's back and salts his top lip. The wind's picking up, whisking dust and ash into his eyes.

They've walked three roads thus far, with only two more turns before they reach Florin's school. If anything, the devastation is worsening. A fact not lost on Gabriela, whose soot-darkened face is now streaked with tears as well as sweat.

Nearby crackles of heavy weaponry set Floyd's nerves on edge. The sight of drones hovering above bombed-out houses exacerbates his anxiety.

When they turn the next corner onto a broad boulevard shorn of most of its trees by the air strike, minds hazed by fumes and heat are swiftly brought into focus. Zombies loiter. The blackened figures stumble from one smouldering ruin to the next. There are at least a hundred in view. That number is rapidly decreasing, however, as two UAVs noisily riddle bodies with large calibre shells. Up ahead, a sidestreet will take the humans away from the carnage, but the right turn is haunted by the undead.

"Need to take cover." Gurdeep continues; a rattle of cannon fire drowns out his second sentence. "I said, or we can go back."

As one, the foursome look over their shoulders. They've been followed, though, by a new collection of monsters. One of the drones must register the zombs' arrival, because it's moving to intercept.

"Dat house?" *We can get into da back garden, den into da next street.* Floyd points at a detached structure to their right, its only structural damage a man-sized hole in the roof, and an integral garage converted into a pile of bricks. He leads the way. Once inside, the singed door is slammed shut.

Gurdeep turns a key in the lock. "Were we followed?"

The teenagers don't look sure, but they shake their heads.

Floyd heads straight down the hall, noting a crimson trail. An old woman's corpse on the floor is the source of the gore. Judging by the shard of glass in her hand and the gaping wound at her throat, she was the architect of her own end. Distracted by the pints of blood, Floyd doesn't see the dead people in the backyard straightaway. "Down! Tangoes!"

Like him, Gurdeep drops to the ground. The children aren't as quick. Floyd risks a quick glance over the kitchen sink: the zombies continue to stand in the sun.

Shit. Trapped. "We'll just 'ave to 'ope da drones take dem out."

"Fuck." Gurdeep rises to a crouch and trains his SA80 on the front door. It's slightly ajar, twitching in the breeze. "Go check upstairs. If it's clear, the kids can go up there, outta the way."

The first floor's rooms are deserted, though the flutter of curtains in the draft from open windows quickens Floyd's pulse. "Clear!" he calls down. With Theo and Gabriela safely upstairs, Floyd and Gurdeep sit, back-to-back, in the hallway. Private Nelson watches the building's rear exit, Private Singh the front. Neither man speaks for a moment. Their ears strain for signs of enemies, but they hear nothing apart from cannon volleys.

Despite the desperation of their position, Floyd takes comfort from the closeness of his friend. If death is imminent, he would rather it took him with Gurd at his side. *Wonder if he finks da same? Probably not.*

"What next?" the Asian asks.

"Dunno, bruv. Survive."

"Yeah, obviously. But what 'bout the tank we just sent for a swim? What 'bout Lena fuckin' Adderley? What 'bout Maguire?"

"Fuck dem. Fuck dem all."

"Don't be a dick, Floyd. We just threw explosives at our own tank —"

"— Not *our* tank. Dem black-wearin' bastards —"

"— Okay, whatever. But either way, findin' 'n' killin' Adderley is our only shot. If we don't, we'll be marked men. Plus she's obviously bad news, causin' all this shit. If we *don't* get her, she could attack again."

"Bullshit. You *know* it's bullshit, Gurd. If she was a proper, legit target, da Army would go after her without all dis cloak 'n' dagger shit. So let's not pretend we be doin' it for any reason other dan savin' our own skins."

"I dunno. I still reckon there must be *some* good reason we've been sent to kill the bitch."

"Dat's your 'company-man' bias talkin'. You put too much faith in dem, bruv. Dere's definitely sometin' dodgy goin' on. Like dese special forces guys. 'Ow da fuck do dey tie into all dis?"

"I don't know, bruv. I just don't know." Gurdeep deflates. "What do *you* reckon we do, then?"

Floyd wipes perspiration and muck from his eyes, then massages the bridge of his nose. "Get dem kids, 'n' get outta dis shithole. We ain't gonna find deir families now."

"Go completely AWOL?"

"Yeah. Fink of it dis way. First of all, should we even be killin' dis Adderley character? Is she actually da bad guy 'ere? Second, even if we *do* kill her, ya reckon da brass'll give us a medal or sometin'? No way. We disobeyed orders dis morning. We shot down dat drone. We put dat tank in da water. Most importantly, we'll 'ave killed Adderley."

"So?" Gurdeep moves forward and looks over his shoulder. "That's a good fing, surely?"

"Dat's where yer wrong, fam." Floyd flinches as a drone gun roars directly outside the house. "We'll be a 'loose end'. What if we talk to da wrong people about da confidential mission we did? Easier just to kill us."

"Now yer bein' paranoid."

"Bruv, we're surrounded by zombies, special forces 'n' armed drones. If dere's ever a time to be paranoid, it's now. Anyway, I wasn't finished. Third point is dis. What's da chances o' findin' Adderley? 'Ow do we know she's not already dead? Buried under a ton o' bricks? We could be lookin' forever 'n' never find 'er."

"I guess so."

"We don't 'ave forever, Gurd. We only been in town five minutes, 'n' dere's bare zombies all over da place. We be lucky to survive another hour. So fuck dis shit. Let's dust. Take da kids 'n' run."

"Deal with the fallout later?"

"'Xactly. Dere might not even be any fallout. If dis disease spreads…"

"The whole country could be fucked. Meaning no brass chasin' us. Fuck it. Let's go." A single tear appears on Gurdeep's cheek. "If it *is* the whole country… my mum 'n' dad…"

It takes all of Floyd's self-control to resist drying his comrade's eye. "So dat's where we'll go, Gurd. Back to London. Back to our ends. Save da peeps dat matter." He glances at the staircase. "An' dese kids."

"They're peeps that matter?"

"Yeah. Dey are to me. Dey've already been through so much. Dey need someone to look out for dem."

A drone spouts destruction outside. Some of its rounds hit the detached building's walls. Then, once the barrage is over, there's a different sound, a whining whirr that gets quieter by the second.

"Gone?" Floyd wonders.

"Let's go check." Gurdeep leads the way, crouching, into the lounge. They creep to its wide bay window and take a look. Apart from the bleeding bodies of numerous zombies, the street is clear.

Theo and Gabriela are summoned. When told of the soldiers' plan to leave town, the teenagers are happy to acquiesce.

"'Ang on," the boy says, "we're only five minutes from Florin 'n' Evie's primary school. Before we leave Mortborough, we should —"

"— Go see. Yer right." Floyd looks each child in the eye. "But ya need to be prepared for da worst. Dey might —"

"Be dead." Gabriela's tone is flat. "We know."

The two army privates cover the youngsters as they lead the way. A couple of minutes later, they're passing a mining museum, the entrance of which is clustered with zombies. A left, a right, and they're at the school. Three quarters of the academy has been flattened, with the remainder scorched by fire. Nevertheless, the kids seem undeterred.

The entrance to the intact quarter is thronged by undead, yet Theo and Gabriela are intent on making entry. Floyd and Gurdeep use grenades to clear the way, then escort the former pupil and his friend from classroom to classroom. They leave with nothing but soot-stained faces and racking coughs for their trouble.

Both are disconsolate. Upon arrival, they accepted their search would probably prove fruitless, but they're crushed all the same. *Poor little fuckers.*

"Time to go," Floyd says, a hand on Gabriela's shoulder as they turn onto Pit Pony Avenue: a row of nineteenth century miners' cottages. "We'll see if we can find a car, eh? One dat ain't burnt to a crisp."

"Put all this behind us." Gurdeep's crouching behind a front yard's wall, using his rifle's telescopic sights to reconnoitre the road ahead. "Hang on." He raises a hand. Motions for everyone to get down. "Fink I've spotted a sniper. Top floor... eighth house on the right... see?"

With his own scope, Floyd watches the window in question. "Is-it?" He ignores the children fidgeting at his side. "Can't — ah, right." Something flashes. "We'll just go 'round. Dere's a street runnin' parallel wiv dis one —"

The cottage's front door opens; both men lower their aims.

Chapter 47 — Jada Blakowska — 15:45

She wipes sweat from her eyes with the loose bedsheet. Then she uses the sheet to wipe her misted breath off the window. *They're not wearin' black.* The words, uttered by her thirty seconds previous, echo around her head. Servicemen wearing standard army gear can be equally as deadly as ones dressed in black. Yet, even so, just a few feet below her, Luke and Brad are moving into the open. They're placing too much significance on the colour of the soldiers fatigues. It'll cost them their lives; Jada will be to blame, because she said, "They're not wearin' black."

All she can do is keep watching the pair of dark-skinned men and shout a warning if they seem about to open fire.

They're already aimin' their rifles, though. How much more 'about to open fire' do you expect 'em to seem, you idiot?

"Need to go an' warn 'em," she mutters to herself. "Before it's too late." Underneath her, the door stops creaking. Luke and Brad will be walking into a hail of bullets any second now, and the camouflaged men will come for her next. The zombies that gave chase from the mine were escaped when she and her four companions ran into the next street then climbed over a fence to double back onto Pit Pony Avenue. These gunmen won't be escaped so easily.

"Is everythin' okay?" Connor's been here the whole time, but his voice still makes Jada jump.

"Who's there?" Evie asks. "Can *I* look?"

"No, just stay sat on the bed. Away from the window." Jada continues to eyeball the two camo-clad men. Save for the twitching of the lighter-skinned man's beard in the wind, they're as still as statues. But one false move, and those big, army-issue assault rifles will spit death. *Shit, they might fire just 'cause Luke an' Brad are carryin' pistols. They're not to know the guns are empty, are they?*

"What's going on?" Lena, who's been watching out of the back bedroom's window to ensure they weren't being surrounded, has entered the front bedroom.

"Shh. Just wait."

Gravel crunches. Looking directly down, Jada sees her two friends. They advance, hands in the air.

"Down on the ground!" the soldier with facial hair yells. "Hands behind your back."

Once Luke and Brad have complied, the bearded man dashes across to the yard beneath Jada, while the taller, darker man covers. *Hang on, is that a kid with him?* Two *kids, boy and girl, older than* — Suddenly, Evie and Connor are at her side.

"Theo!" the former shouts. She tears away, with Connor and Jada close behind. He almost catches Evie in the cottage's short hallway, but she squirms away and flies through the front door.

"Freeze!" The black guy raises his rifle.

"Evie!" the boy behind him yells. "It's okay! Floyd, Gurdeep, it's okay. These are good guys."

Introductions are given; brief stories are shared. Theo and Evie are delighted to be reunited, though the joy is quickly dampened when they learn of their parents' fates. Of the ten present, only Lena is silent. The two privates, Floyd and Gurdeep are nearly as guarded. Strangely, they regard the two women with the most suspicion. They seem about to speak when Evie exclaims and points in the direction of the mine: zombies are coming.

Everyone runs. Gabriela suggests heading back to the canal and following it out of town. Theo reminds her of the black-garbed infantry unit stationed near the boathouse, but she says they can flee into the quarry if need be. The others back her.

The boat commandeered earlier has been scuppered, meaning they have to walk. But on the brighter side, most of the men-in-black have redeployed, leaving a base camp of half a dozen bored-looking operatives behind.

Shaking her head, Jada photographs the half-crashed, half-sunk tank. Theo's tale of its demise impresses the younger children in particular.

It's mental, how much we've all been through in the last day an' a bit. At least I've got some evidence of Government shenanigans now, an' we have Lena. Plus Luke's got Connor back. An' Evie's safe, thank God.

Walking the towpath, the group encounter little resistance. Privates Singh and Nelson are more than capable of defeating the scattered pairs and trios of undead, headshotting the creatures before they pose a threat. The two squaddies are reticent about their own past and future, merely stating they've been separated from their unit. They've not said as much, but they seem to have adopted the role of protectors of Theo and Gabriela. Right now, this means they're doing what they do best: waging war.

Drones continue to criss-cross the sky over Mortborough, Walkley and Swinford, but the black-suits are nowhere to be seen .The sun grows stronger as the wind gets weaker. The reek of rotting biomass sharpens, no longer masked by that of smoke. Stomachs rumble. Kids gripe about sore limbs and thirst. Conversation between the adults is at a premium; everyone is too weary for small talk, too traumatised to discuss the horrors they've seen.

Everyone except Jada, that is. Despite the addition of much-needed firepower, in the form of Singh and Nelson, their party is far from safe. However, her journalistic mind is already considering the bigger picture. She's eager to exploit Lena and expose the Government players responsible for the outbreak. Thinking Brad will be her best ally in this respect, she falls into step next to him. "They're still headin' towards Mortborough, aren't they?" She nods at the latest monster to appear in the distance, just as a shot from Floyd stops it for good.

"Yeah. Fuckers keep comin'." The man's voice is apathetic.

"I believe they're drawn to the source of the chemical." It's the first time Lena's spoken since they were in the cottage. "The Resurrex, I mean."

"Yeah?" Jada steps on a large stone, turning her injured ankle. Ignoring the pain, she asks, "What makes you say that?"

"Just something Doc— I mean, just a thought. Probably wrong, I'm no expert."

"A thought of whose? A doctor, you were gonna say?" *She's exhausted. Probably concussed. An' she nearly let out the truth by accident. Need to keep pushin'.*

"No. I… I wasn't going to say —"

"— 'Document', then? Was that what you were gonna say?"

"No. I… I'm just tired, that's all."

"Cut the bullshit, Lena."

"Excuse me?" The exec's tone becomes more haughty. "I haven't the faintest idea what you're talking about, Jada."

"I don't believe you." Jada lowers her voice; their chat is piquing the others' attention. "A doctor gave you their theory, didn't they? But you don't want us to know that, 'cause you were supposed to be 'corporate only'."

Slowly but steadily, the truth is revealed.

By the end, Ms Adderley appears equally relieved, ashamed and afraid. She weeps as she tells of Aslam's end, and the tears seem genuine.

So absorbed is Jada that she doesn't realise that Floyd and Gurdeep haven't fired their rifles for a couple of minutes. A sudden flurry of shots kills the zombs that'd got too close for comfort, and it startles the reporter. Everyone has stopped walking, rapt by Lena's tale.

The four children are confused, to varying degrees.

Floyd is both fascinated and repelled.

Luke is harder to read: he's shocked but also anxious, no doubt dreading the potential fallout.

His disquiet is only made worse by Brad's expression. The smaller man glowers at the confessor with almost as much naked aggression as earlier, in the mine. He doesn't take kindly to Luke standing between himself and Adderley, though for the time being, he doesn't act.

Only one person shows no reaction. Private Gurdeep Singh's face is blank. It's so neutral that, when he raises his rifle, no one responds in time.

Apart from Luke. He dives into the soldier as the trigger is pulled. The rifle crack echoes.

Lena gasps, goes to ground, yelps in pain.

Winded, Gurdeep stumbles.

Now Floyd steps in, his gun held like a club.

Intercepting, Brad seizes Floyd's rifle with both hands. It fires once before it's wrested free.

"Stop!" Jada screams. "Just stop, please!"

Floyd punches Brad on the jaw. The rifle falls, hitting the footpath at the same time as the man who dropped it. Luke tries to scoop up the weapon, but the Caribbean soldier kicks it away whilst unholstering a handgun.

"Everybody! Down on your knees." Floyd fires a warning shot in the air. "Gurdeep. Gurdeep! You okay, fam? Da fuck, Gurd... oh, no." He squats by his friend, cradles his head. "No, Gurd, ya gonna be okay, fam..." Almost in disbelief, he looks at the blood on his fingers. It comes from the back of the Sikh's head. More pulses from the man's open mouth, soaking the black beard.

Eyes wide, lips quivering, Private Floyd Nelson stands tall. The pistol shakes in his sticky scarlet hands.

Chapter 48 — Lena Adderley — 16:20

"So if you weren't going to listen to my concerns," Dr Aslam rails, "if you were always planning to push ahead with Resurrex, then why bother meeting with me?"

She has a point. Lena tries for a rebuttal, something pithy or inspiring, perhaps, but her lips aren't working.

"What will you say when your government cronies ask if it's safe?"

They won't ask, because they don't care. Nor do I, really. All I want is recognition: from the industry; from the media; the public. And most of all, from Dad. Of course, such attention will become a curse if the chemical proves ineffective or dangerous. But that's the risk you take in business, isn't it?

"Do you not understand how bad this could get?" Aslam is leaning across the table now, her fists clenched, the finest sheen of spittle on her chin. Teeth bared, pointy and brilliant white. Her eyes glowing red… "It's an extremely volatile chemical. If it reacts badly with some kind of factor we haven't considered…"

Shut the fuck up, Little Miss Smart-arse. No one gives a shit as long as we all get paid.

Now the scientist's is reaching for Lena, long nails wickedly sharp. "Wake up, Lena! Come on, stay with us. Stay with us, for fucksake. You're not dyin' on us now!" Aslam's lips are moving, but it's not her voice. It's… it's… *Jada Blakowska.*

Her eyes snap open. She whimpers; her right calf is on fire.

A tall black man is standing, shouting. His words are muffled, as though he's underwater. *Floyd.* Two rifles are strapped to his back, but he's holding a handgun, with another at his hip, and he's pointing it at the group of people on their knees. At his feet, on the canal towpath, there's a dead man with a beard. *Private Gurdeep Singh.* Slowly, the ranting soldier's voice clarifies, and the gun in his hands becomes less of a blur. "He's dead 'cause o' you lot! 'N' dat bitch on da floor dere. All da shit she done, 'n' ya took *her* side!"

"Didn't take no one's side," a man argues. Lena wants to turn her head to see who it is, but she's too weak. It takes all of her strength just to keep her eyes open. "Didn't want *anyone* t' get shot. We weren't t' know he was gonna freak out 'n' start pointin' 'is gun at people. Even then, we just wanted 'im t' calm down. We didn't want anyone t' get 'urt."

"Yeah, well. Someone did get 'urt, didn't dey? My friend, my squadmate, my… my… *Fuck!* I should kill da fuckin' lot o' ya, right now."

"You won't do that, Floyd." *Is that Jada? Yes.* "'Cause you're a good man, Floyd. A good man, under a lot of stress, who's seen some awful shit, done his best to deal with it, risked his life for a coupla kids, an' ended up losin' his best friend. But a *good man*."

Lena's vision is wavering again. The urge to fall back to sleep is stronger even than the pain in her leg. *If I drift off again, I may never wake up…* She attempts to push herself up onto her elbows, but she may as well be trying to pull that tank out of the canal.

Suddenly, Floyd is looking her way. "Don't fuckin' move, Adderley. Don't give me an excuse. Shoulda listened to Gurd 'n' killed ya the second I saw ya. But I was too much of a pussy. Now he's gone… *Fuck!*" He covers half of his face with one hand while using the other to keep the pistol trained on his prisoners.

"Floyd. Bro." Brad clears his throat. "I feel ya. I lost someone yesterday. My fuckin' daughter, man. Worse than losin' a friend, right? 'N' I 'ad t' kill her myself, too. Did I wanna take revenge? Course I did. Still do. Against 'er on the ground. Against *everybody*. But killin' Adderley, shit, killin' anyone, won't bring back yer buddy. Won't bring back my daughter."

"Only things we should be killin' are those fuckin' zombies," Luke adds. "'N' there's still plenty of 'em about, can ya not smell 'em? They could get 'ere any minute now, so we really don't wanna be 'angin 'round —"

"— No. Shut up." Floyd's face clears, as if he's found clarity. "I ain't gonna kill 'er. I'm gonna take 'er back to da army. Like Gurdeep wanted. He was right all along, so I'm gonna do what he said. That's what we're doin'. All of us. You're comin' too, so I have witnesses, 'n' shit." Ignoring the others' protests, he approaches Lena. He stoops, slips an arm under her neck.

She cringes, but she doesn't have the strength to fight. When Floyd begins to haul her upright, a lightning bolt of pain strikes her lower leg. All becomes dark.

"I trust your judgment, Lena." With his now-customary half-smile, half-grimace, Grant Adderley sits up straighter in bed. He looks mildly ridiculous in pyjamas.

"I usually trust my own, Dad." She pours him another glass of water. "But this Dr Aslam, she has such a good reputation in her field. And she's so damn sure we've got it wrong!"

"What do her peers say?"

As I said five minutes ago: "They disagree. But she's best qualified."

"I trust your judgment, Lena."

You've already said that, Dad. "Thanks. Everything's going well, though. The government contract's going to make us multinational. You'll have a legacy to be proud of."

"Excellent. I knew you'd do well. Always had faith in you."

"But we're being careful, doing things safely, protecting the company's reputation. We won't fall into the same trap as we did last time, I promise."

"Last time?" The old man yawns.

Oh god, oh fuck, that hurts so much. She's upright now. Everything is a haze, all of her senses dulled by pain. Although the sun is bright, she feels cold. Her surroundings – the canal, the footpath, the bridge in the distance – seem familiar, but she can't be sure if she's been here before in person.

People are arguing. There's a deep bass voice, the angriest. The others, two men and a woman, speak in a pleading tone, at length, though Lena can't make out their words. She can smell blood, and she can taste blood.

Suddenly, she lurches forward; darkness returns.

Dad's wearing his suit. He's sat at the antique desk in his wood panelled office, occupying the space like he's never been away. The bewildered expression he's worn for the last few months has been replaced by the knowing smile that could be endearing or menacing depending on the beholder. "Take a seat, Lena." His tone is cool and brooks no opposition.

He's got better! His doctors were wrong, unlike hers: Sofia Aslam.

She sits without a word. For a moment, she holds her father's gaze; then both laugh. Neither Adderley is partial to power games, so they get straight to the point.

"There's no point beating around the bush." He coughs suddenly and with vigour. "This Resurrex thing is a problem. A big fucking problem. The country's overrun by zombies. Our share price has plummeted. And this researcher of yours, this Asian girl, she's giving interviews left, right and centre, saying you ignored her about the risks."

"I didn't *ignore* her. I took her advice on board, made a judgment, took a risk, like *you* always taught me."

"So I did. But do you remember what else I always said?"

"What, Dad?"

"That if you take a risk, and it goes wrong, then you have to face the consequences."

"Which are?"

"You're grounded, for a month. Consider —"

"— Oh, Dad, come on!" She pouts. "That's so unfair."

"That's the end of it. And let me... let..." His next sentence is swallowed by a coughing fit. He's soon spluttering blood and mucus all over the bureau and a horrified Lena. Within a minute, he collapses, face down, across his desk. Thirty seconds later, he's straightening up. Eyes full of malevolence, his bloody mouth slack.

Zombie-Dad growls and leaps over the furniture; his screaming daughter reels away.

"Yes, sir. I have her secured, over." The man's deep voice is tense.

Her eyes are suddenly wide.

Jada's there. She smiles, a gesture returned by Lena. There's regret on the younger woman's face, pity too. "Don't worry," the reporter says. "I've given you something for the pain. It should kick in soon."

"Already has." The businesswoman takes in her surroundings. They're in a pub named The Wharfstar, which overlooks a basin in the canal. Her right lower leg is freshly bandaged; there's an open first aid kit on the low table by the couch, next to a small empty bottle, which must've contained painkillers. The astringent smell of antiseptics is heady. *Where did they get morphine from?* "How did we get here?"

"Luke and Brad carried you."

"Where are the children?"

"Which ones? Connor and Evie are sleeping upstairs. They're both exhausted, poor buggers. Theo and Gabriela are in the bar, keeping an eye on the main road."

"I could take her to da special forces unit, sir." Floyd's outside, but there's an open window behind the sofa on which Lena lies. "Dey're wearin' black, sir. Dey're all over Mortborough. Surely you've seen dem on cam feeds —"

He falls silent again, and Lena and Jada share a look of confusion.

"Understood, sir. And until den, sir?"

"They don't know who the black-suits are," Jada whispers. "Or if they do, they're pretendin' they don't."

Lena frowns. "Aren't they all on the same side, sort of?"

"Yes, sir. I… Are you sure you don't want me — Sir. Certainly, sir. Over and out." The private's sudden silence is ominous, but the opiates in Lena's system keep her calm. When Floyd unleashes a stream of expletives and overturns an outdoor table, smashing glass, the first icy fingers of fear creep along her spine.

Biting her lip, Jada stands to look out of the window. "I wish I'd never pushed you into the Aslam confession. Everythin's gone to shit since."

"You're a journalist. You did your job. The truth should be told, whatever the consequences. The truth should be respected, listened to. If I'd listened to Dr Aslam, to the truth, we wouldn't be in this mess. So if I have to face the music, I will."

"Judgin' by Private Nelson's reaction to his orders, that music could be on the way." Jada cranes her neck to watch Floyd; he must be moving around outside. Though anxious to keep watch on him herself, Lena's still too drained.

A door opens. In comes the soldier, followed by Brad and Luke.

"Just tell us what you're plannin'!" the former says.

Luke's trying to get in front of Floyd. "Slow down, mate. Let's just talk about this!"

"Fuck off!" Nelson raises his pistol. "Both of you, back da fuck up. You too," he says as Jada moves to intercept. "Sit down, everyone." When no one complies, he chambers a round in his weapon. "I said, sit da fuck down." His face is taut; his camouflaged tunic soaked in sweat. "Don't test me. Do not fucking test me right now."

Luke, Brad and Jada take seats around Lena.

For a moment, Floyd does nothing, says nothing. Apart from the steady rise and fall of his chest and the flicker of his eyes from one person to the next, he is motionless. Eventually, his gaze settles on Lena Adderley.

"Floyd. Will you listen to me for a second?" Jada's voice is serene. "And we'll all listen to you as well."

The young man remains silent, but his shoulders loosen a touch.

Although the other two males present seem eager to speak, they seem to sense that their journalist friend will have better luck.

"What's goin' on, Floyd?"

"What's goin' on? Dat bitch dere started dis whole ting. If it wasn't for 'er, me 'n' my boy Gurdeep would still be chillin' in da barracks. Now I'm 'ere, in dis northern shithole, 'n' Gurdeep's fuckin' *dead*."

"It was Brad who went for your gun, Floyd. Not Lena." Jada ignores a glare from the man she's just accused. "But even Brad doesn't deserve to be punished, 'cause it was an *accident*."

"I know dat! An accident dat wouldn't 'ave 'appened wivout *her*."

"But you know so little about 'her'. Certainly not enough to kill her."

"I know she's a terrorist!" He speaks with ferocity, but there's doubt in his mind.

Lena winces as she forces herself to sit up. Tinnitus and nausea threaten, but she needs to fight for her life, so adrenaline compensates. "Floyd," she croaks.

Jada hands her a glass of water, while Private Nelson scowls.

"Floyd. I am *not* a terrorist. If I were a terrorist, why was I found looking after two children? Surely I would've fled as soon as the deed was done."

"Perhaps you 'ad regrets."

"No. I *do* have regrets, but not because I destroyed by home town deliberately. Because I destroyed it *carelessly*."

"Obviously yer just gonna deny it, ain't ya?"

"I understand that you're hurt. Your friend has died, and I must take some of the blame for that, because it's my company's chemical which caused the outbreak that led to you and Private Singh coming here. So, yes, blame me. *I* blame me, for fucksake! But blame me for the right thing. For recklessly causing the deaths of thousands, not for purposely *murdering* thousands."

"Where ya get this 'terrorist' thing from, Floyd?" Luke asks.

"None o' your fuckin' business," the squaddie replies, but with less venom than earlier.

"The Army are lyin' to you," says Jada. "They want you to kill Lena, don't they? They told you she's a terrorist, didn't they?"

"But you doubted it, right?" Lena has just about enough strength to raise her eyebrows. "That's why Gurdeep was going to take me out, but you hesitated."

It's all sinking in. Their arguments chip away at his resolve, replacing conviction with uncertainty. *He's a good man. He didn't have to let the kids tag along, or help them search the school, did he?*

That doesn't stop him from raising his handgun and pulling the trigger, however.

Chapter 49 — Theo Callaghan — 17:15

The gunshot silences both teenagers.

"I told you!" the girl hisses. "I told you things were gonna go crazy. Let's just get Evie an' run!"

Blood running cold, the boy climbs off the window seat. *The guy seemed okay. He was the one who actually wanted to 'elp us. But since Gurdeep got shot, he's been mental.*

Theo takes a few tentative steps towards The Wharfstar's main entrance. To the back of the public house, where the grown-ups have just been arguing.

What to do now? Grab Evie 'n' leg it, or find out what's goin' on?

He looks at Gabriela, who points up. "The kids!" she mouths as they continue to creep into the restaurant area.

Too late. The door marked 'PRIVATE', which leads to first floor staff accommodation, is wide open. His sister and her new friend are already passing the dumb waiter, hand-in-hand.

More shots, these ones automatic, two distinct barrages of rifle fire. Smaller weapons fire individual shots. Glass splinters. Spent cartridges tinkle on the ground. People shout.

"Evie!" Theo calls. When she turns, he signals for her to retreat, but she shakes her head. *Little shit!* He breaks into a jog, as does Gabriela.

They have to turn a corner to enter the dining area. At the back of the space, overlooking the canal basin, four humans are doing battle. The other, already injured, is passing fresh magazines to those in need. Beyond them, outside the pub, the dead are on the march. Floyd is shooting with his SA80. Jada's using Gurdeep's. Luke and Brad have a pistol each. Lena's as pale as cream, but she's doing what she can. The noise is chastening, the reek of cordite and sour bodies overwhelming.

While Gabriela grabs Connor, Theo seizes a gaping Evie by the shoulder and drags her back into the bar area. "Stay here!" he orders.

The children nod meekly and stay put.

Back into the eatery the teens go. Theo doesn't know how, but perhaps they can help. The horde is getting closer: monsters are being shot on the window ledges now, spilling crimson and grey brains on interior furniture rather than the sun-baked terrace outside.

"Look!" Gabriela points at a fire exit. The door is breached; zombies are squirming through, heedlessly excoriating their arms, legs and faces on jagged spikes of glass.

None of the adults have noticed. They're too busy loading and firing. Pulse pounding in his ears, Theo scans the tables. An axe. A fire extinguisher. A sledgehammer. He retrieves the former, Gabriela the latter. With every instinct compelling him to do the opposite, he heads for the fire door.

Slipping on its own blood, the first freak, once a waitress, takes the axe head between its eyes. The sound is as satisfying as it is disturbing. Theo pulls the blade free, showering his own cheek with warm wetness. He chops at another, cuts deep into its chest. One next to it spins away. Skull shattered by Gabriela's hammer. Between them, the youngsters slaughter half a dozen invaders, then push a table up against the smashed fire door.

"Out! All out!" Lena yells.

There are still at least fifty zombies outside. A minority are copying those Theo and Gabriela beat back, heading for entrances other than the big bay window at the pub's rear. Already, some are banging on the front door.

"Stop firin', 'n' up the stairs!" Floyd orders.

Easier t' defend one staircase than every door 'n' window downstairs. 'Specially when you've nearly run outta ammo.

Everyone surges towards the staff-only door. Connor and Evie join them, and they fly upstairs. A corpulent man in his fifties – the pub landlord, perhaps – is lying in a pool of blood, blocking the doorway to the residential area, keeping the self-locking door open. Luke and Brad manhandle the corpse out of the way and let it roll down the stairs. Floyd uses his pistol to repulse the pair of undead that appear below in the meantime.

The heavy door is slammed shut behind them, lessening the stench from the dead body. Everyone but Floyd breathes a sigh of relief.

"Need to block up this door," the soldier says, already pulling a leather sofa from a lounge. "Heavy stuff. Fridges, freezers, 'n' shit."

A thud from the security door means the dead have started their assault. *It's a strong door, though, innit? Proper thick 'n' 'eavy.*

Theo and Gabriela join in, helping the grown-ups with the lifting and dragging. Evie and Connor collect weapons together: knives, hammers, screwdrivers, rolling pins. Plus food, for they need to keep nourished to survive. The battery to the door intensifies, but the steel and wood structure holds firm.

Now all they can do is wait, and rest. Escape is impossible, so their only hope is that the undead are distracted by easier pickings before they gain entry. Because if they get in, everyone will die. This certitude of Theo's is not pessimism. He's sat on a box room window ledge, staring through barred windows at the sun-dappled canal, and he can see more dead people heading for the pub. They arrive sporadically, in ones and twos. But they never stop coming.

When he was in the townhouse cellar in the early hours of this morning, Theo decided the zombies are like fire. All-consuming, lethal, feasting on everything in their path. He's changed his mind; they're more like water. Getting into every nook and cranny, drowning life, destroying property. They're inevitable. Rivers carve canyons through the strongest rock, and eventually, given enough time, the hellish fiends on the stairs will burst into the pub's living space and tear the survivors to pieces.

I should go 'n' spend time with Evie. If I'm scared, she's bound t' be shittin' 'erself. He feels frozen, however, paralysed by fear.

"You okay?" Gabriela asks from the doorway, making him jump. She takes a seat on a plastic chair – one of the few items of furniture considered too small and light to include in the barricade.

"Yeah. I guess." He smiles sadly. *I'm gonna die soon. We're all gonna die soon, but I still don't 'ave the balls t' tell 'er 'ow I feel. Too scared o' bein' friend-zoned.* He grins for a second; they're won't even be 'people-zones' if this plague spreads, let alone 'friend-zones.'

"What's funny?"

"Nothin'. Are we gonna die?"

"Everybody dies."

"No, I mean *now*. Are we gonna die now?"

"I don't know. But in case we are, let's go an' sit with everyone else, hey?"

"Okay." He groans as he stands; he's aching like his dad used to, before he died and turned. In the lounge, everyone looks exhausted and hopeless. Unsurprisingly, Lena looks the worst. As her bandage gets redder, her cheeks become more insipid. Floyd seems to have calmed down, but perhaps he'll resume his offensive against the Evolve CEO when they escape.

If we escape.

The banging on the door has been of a consistent volume and frequency for the last five minutes. Until now. Suddenly, it's a crunch instead of a thump, as if penetration has been achieved. As the closest to the lounge entrance, Theo looks out into the corridor. The dent has become a cavity. Said cavity is only small, but it enlarges with every blow. *Shit.*

Floyd joins him in the hallway. "Is dere access to da roof?" the soldiers asks no one in particular.

Most of the group stay silent; perhaps they're too mentally-fatigued to deal with another crisis so soon after the last. But looking at Evie's trembling face lends Theo a resolve that'd all but deserted him a few moments ago.

Gabriela stands, her jaw proud, wiry body full of energy. "I saw a skylight in the roof when we got here. If we can get into the loft…"

"Right." Floyd claps his hands. "Wakey wakey, everyone. Wiv da amount o' shit we put in front o' dat door, it'll take a while for dem ugly motherfuckers to get in. Me 'n' da kids gonna check dis loft out. See if we can get out dat way. I need you lot sharp. Ready. In case da zombies make it through while I's up dere. Come on, look lively."

Gabriela finds the attic hatch in the kitchen, bizarrely enough. It's stiff and needs a couple of hammer strikes before it opens. There's no ladder, but tall, sinewy Floyd – with the hammer tucked into one of his pockets – pulls himself up with little difficulty. "Find a chair, or sometin," he calls down. "Not one from da barricade, obvs."

Theo heads to the box room in which he contemplated his own mortality, just five minutes ago. He grabs the chair, goes back to the kitchen, nods at a sledgehammer-holding Luke as he passes the exit, gives Evie a wink like one of Dad's. Now the teenaged boy has purpose. *We're gonna get outta this place. We're gonna make it.*

The chair he brings is needed for Floyd to reach the skylight, apparently. The loft's only lightbulb is broken, the soldier complains. Craning his neck, Theo gazes into the gloom. He sees nothing, but hears a couple of whacks, along with the jangle of breaking glass and the grating sound of glass shards being cleared from the frame.

Then Floyd's face appears at the opening, his teeth startlingly white. "Here, Gabriela. Take dis chair, stand on it, den I'll pull you up, while Theo gives you a push. Actually, Theo, go tell da others da plan first. We'll climb up, one at a time. Den out onto da roof." He passes down the chair.

One by one, everyone ascends to the attic, then up onto the roof. Halfway through the process, there's a crash from the first floor as the blockage gives way. The sound of footsteps beneath them galvanises weary arms and legs. Lena almost passes out when a combination of Luke, Brad and Floyd convey her through the trapdoor; her calf dressing drips scarlet by the time they're all sat on the warm roof tiles.

The wind is delicious on Theo's clammy brow. His arms ache, but he feels good. Now all they have to do get down to the ground, which is now free of enemies – they're all inside. The Wharfstar. A gate almost directly below them gives access to the water. More of the canal is visible from this height: around the next bend, about fifty paces away, there's a barge. It won't be fast, but —

"Shit." Jada's pointing in the opposite direction, at the main road.

Others echo her curse. While there are only ten of the black-suits in the car park, they are heavily-armed and moving quickly.

Theo's head drops.

Chapter 50 — Luke Norman — 17:05

"Freeze! Do *not* move!" Perhaps the mask distorts the short, stocky man's voice, because he sounds foreign. The barrel of his rifle, pointing in the survivors' direction, sends a message of its own. "You will disarm. You will immediately come down from the roof."

Floyd nods. He tosses his rifle, but not towards the squad of black-clad troops. It lands with a clatter on the terrace between the pub and the canal. While everyone else follows suit, the private indicates Lena, who's now verging on delirium. "We have a casualty."

"That is not our problem. You are now our prisoners. You will comply, or you will die. Is this understood?"

"Yeah. Loud 'n' clear. You need to know, dough, dat dis pub is full of zombies."

The mysterious officer makes no reply.

"Zombies. You know, da undead."

After ten full seconds of silence, the man-in-black drones, "Immediately proceed to the ground, or we will open fire. We will launch grenades, so you cannot hide."

"Right," says Jada, "we do as they say, but slowly —"

"— Yeah, then get shot?" Brad shakes his head. "They got no intention o' takin' us prisoner —"

"— No way o' transportin' us," Luke agrees. "They just wanna get us down t' make us easier t' shoot."

"Good point." Floyd grits his teeth. "I's not goin' down wivout —"

"— If you'd just let me finish." Jada huffs. "We make our way down, *slowly*, an' we find some way of lurin' the zombies outta the pub in the meantime. Set 'em on the soldiers."

"Good plan, Jada." *She's the smartest one 'ere by a country mile. But...* "'Ow do we lure the zombs out?"

"Throw me down." Suddenly Lena's lucid, with all of her trademark snootiness restored. "I owe it to all of you."

"Don't be fuckin' stupid," Brad scorns. "Yer a bitch, but we ain't feedin' ya t' the zombs."

"Not yet." Floyd looks serious.

"We need you, anyway," Jada says. "Evidence against the Government."

Brad nods. "Good point."

"Gotta be another way," Theo says.

"You have ten seconds to make your decision." The officer in black barks. "Then we fire. Ten. Nine. Eight."

"Okay, okay!" Jada waves her hands in the air. "We need to get down on the other side, by the canal. There's a garage there we can climb on."

"Very well." The officer signals for two of his men to circumnavigate The Wharfstar in order to oversee the descent.

The survivors begin the hazardous journey over the pitched roof. As Luke and Brad support Lena, the former notices his son staring at the injured woman's leg. Her bandage is now a claret-stained rag, her right shoe dripping blood onto the dry tiles. Beneath them, floorboards rumble, which means the undead are in the loft. Some are still downstairs in the main pub area, however.

Connor gets Evie's attention as they reach the apex; they both hurry to the edge of the slates.

"Be careful!" Luke warns. *Supposed t' be takin' it slow. Yeah, but what's the point if we don't think of a way o' lurin' the freaks out?*

"Look!" Evie points. The two younger children are excited.

"What?" Luke leaves Lena with Brad and Jada and heads for the edge of the roof. All he can see is the beer garden, the towpath to the canal and the water itself. The two black-suits are watching; they look impatient.

"Lena's blood trail," Connor replied. "Goes from the canal path, over the grass, up onto those flags, between the tables —"

"Yeah, we can see that," says Theo, "but who gives a shit? We're about t' be —"

"— All the wet foot prints follow the trail, dumb-ass," Evie retorts. "They're attracted to blood."

Connor nods vigorously. "They can smell it in our bodies. That's why they come fer us. But when it's out in the open, when someone's bleedin', it sends 'em extra-crazy."

"Down! Now!" one of the paramilitaries yells. "Off the roof, or we shoot."

"Lena!" Jada begins.

"I know," the CEO replies. Grimacing, she peels the soggy dressing from her shin. She bites her lip and lets out no more than whimper. After doing so, she passes the soiled article to Jada and lies back on the roof, panting.

"I count to three!" a black-suit yells. "Then I fire grenade onto roof!"

While Floyd approaches the edge to give a thumb-up, Jada drops the bandage off the side of the pub roof. It lands with a moist slap by the entrance to the smoking enclosure.

"We comin' now," the private promises. He makes a show of looking for a safe way to climb down to the garage.

"Hurry!" the vocal para urges.

A window smashes somewhere under their feet. *Here we go*. The first snarling zombie flies into view at the side of the pub. From above, the once-female creature is almost comical in its confusion. Soon, a second appears, then a third, and all three scramble towards the rear of the building, as though controlled remotely. Luke follows them to join Floyd, who's now abandoned his deception act.

A soldier calls a warning. Rifles fire. Rounds strike wood, glass, brick, plastic and greenery. Bodies as well, but too many shots go awry. The former woman takes one to the chest and drops like a stone, its pink hair fanned out on the terrace. The other two monsters, though, fall on the closest soldier. Soldier two riddles all three – his dying comrade and the undead pair – with bullets.

Meanwhile, the remaining eight soldiers are coming to assist. Just as they arrive in the beer garden, a dozen zombies emerge from The Wharfstar. The paramilitaries are ready; they fire in controlled bursts. But more enemies are coming, from the front of the building, from each side. Even grenade launchers can't prevent them being overwhelmed. The barrel-chested commander is the last to succumb, though he kills at least five zombies in his agonising final minutes.

Helluva way to go. Jesus.

Luke looks away, but he can still hear the tearing sounds and screams. He pulls Connor away from the lip of the roof, hugs him close.

"What we gonna do now?" the boy asks.

"Dunno, son." *The soldiers are dead, 'n' now we're stuck wi' the zombies.*

Floyd's staring at the feasting dead. "If we can get dem rifles —"

"— 'N' 'ow the fuck d'ya suggest we do that?" asks Brad.

"Fuck knows, bruv."

"I thought the men-in-black'd put up a better fight," confesses Jada. "Take more o' the zombies out. But there's still loads left."

"At least there's less in the loft," Luke observes, for the footsteps below have reduced in number. "We should be able t' fight off the few that do work out 'ow t' get up 'ere."

Theo and Gabriela have just returned from checking the opposite side of the pub, above the kitchen entrance. "We might not get the chance," the former says. "They're startin' t' climb the walls."

Floyd goes back to the edge facing the canal. "Same 'ere. Dey're slow, but dey'll get 'ere at some point."

Looking out onto the smoking area, Luke spots the first zombie climber. "What about the front?"

"We'll go look," says Gabriela. The two teens scale the roof and disappear over the other side. A minute later, they're back. "There's no climbers," she says breathlessly. "But there are more of them comin' from the main road."

Everyone lets out a curse or two. Apart from Lena, who's now out cold and deathly white. Luke doesn't want to look at her leg, but he reckons it'll get infected. From where will they get medication?

What the fuck, dickhead? We're not even gonna be alive long enough fer her wound t' go bad. We'll be dead in an hour, tops. Better t' go like Lena. Slip into unconsciousness 'n' never wake up.

"Get a grip, Luke," he whispers to himself. He can't give up now; he has Connor to think about. *And Jada.* He's barely had a moment to consider his feelings for the attractive, warm, intelligent journalist, but the prospect of harm befalling her appals him.

He looks at the rest of the group. They all share similar expressions, ones that speak of extreme fatigue, hopelessness and loss rather than determination or the will to survive. "Come on, guys. There's gotta be somethin' we can do." *But what?* "As soon as we give up mentally, we're as good as dead. So… don't give up! We've all survived worse than this, right? Listen… if we can just get t' the water, there's a barge not far away."

"'Ow do we get t' the water, bro?" Brad asks.

"If we 'ad rifles like deirs." Floyd nods in the general direction of the annihilated crew of black-suits. "Under-barrel grenade launchers, right dere."

"Don't *you* have grenades?" Jada asks.

"All gone."

"Don't you have explosives, like what Gurdeep used on the tank?" says Gabriela.

"Dey don't just give dem to everyone."

"'Ang on," says Evie. "Can anyone else 'ear that?"

Everyone shrugs, apart from Theo, who chuckles. "She's got *sick* hearin'."

"I know what she means." Connor wriggles away from his father and creeps to the roof edge. "It's a boat!"

Luke dashes to his son and pulls him back just as a zombie hand grasps the gable end. He uses his sledgehammer to pulverise the blackening fingers. A second blow on the freak's head sends it crashing to the ground. Another is on the verge. Brad's there, though, chopping down to sever a boy zomb's arm. Floyd uses a combat knife in a similar manner; Jada's employing the butt of an empty rifle to bash faces and appendages.

"Look!" Evie and Connor are becoming more agitated, and not by the siege before them. "It's Josh! And Ashara!" adds the former.

After smashing away another undead acrobat, Luke shields his eyes from the sun. *They're right! Josh 'n' Ashara, in some sorta speedboat. Pullin' up on the canal like we're off on a boat trip!*

Brad and Jada are whooping with joy.

"Still need to get down, dough," says Floyd, wiping his knife on his trousers before replacing it in its sheath. He pulls Gurdeep's sidearm from his waistband. "Saved one bullet for m'self. Just in case." He aims downwards, at the beer garden. "So I could go 'n' join Gurd in da afterlife, worst came to worst, ya get me? Everyone, get da fuck down."

Luke frowns but obeys, as do the rest of the guys. *What's he gonna —*

The pistol's report is drowned out by a boom. Or, rather, a cluster of booms. Floyd ducks and covers his eyes; debris rains on the prostrate survivors.

On his feet again, Luke checks the results below. Not all of the zombies are dead, but many are, and some have been incapacitated, their legs or arms amputated.

"What the fuck was in that bullet?" asks Luke, eyes slits against drifting dust and the lowering sun.

"One of dem MIBs had four grenades left for his launcher. Still in his belt. So I hit one. It blew. So did da rest." Floyd hops down onto the garage roof before anyone can protest, then descends to the terrace. He scoops up an assault rifle and headshots two singed zombies lurching his way. "Come on down," he calls to the rest. "I'll cover." Another dead man stumbles the private's way and takes a slug between the eyes for its trouble.

"He's pretty cool," Luke says, with a half-grin.

"Not as cool as you." Jada gives him arm a squeeze. "That speech you gave was pretty rousing stuff."

The compliment leaves Luke glowing. "Your plan, though. Lure the zombies out. It worked out alright in the end."

She smiles in return.

Soon enough, they're all aboard the boat, chugging away from the few zombies that survived the battle. Lena's suffering, but they've managed to re-bind her leg. Getting her down from the roof was tricky, but they made it. They survived another day.

"How'd ya know we'd be 'ere?" Luke asks Joshua Gould, who looks to be enjoying his stint as boatsman.

"It was Ashara's idea." Gould smiles. "She's a smart cookie, that one." He regards the young woman, who's talking to the children on the other side of the boat, with fondness. "Remember this morning, before you left? I said the waterways could be useful. So, hoping you listened, we were checking CCTV feeds of waterside places. There's a little boathouse up the canal, and we saw people in there. Was that you guys?"

"That was us," says Theo.

"I noticed a guy with a beard, too."

Floyd turns away from everyone to watch the water they leave behind.

"Long story," Jada murmurs.

"Anyway, we didn't know if it was anything to do with you, but we'd lost contact —"

"— Radio battery went —" Brad explains.

"— So we thought we'd take a chance. Good thing we did, eh?"

"Too right." Luke glances at Connor, who's laughing at something Ashara's saying. *Never lettin' you outta my sight again, kid.* "Where ya get the boat from?"

"Crawford Water Park's not far from the Centre. Simple job when you know what you're doing." Gould pats the steering wheel. "This boat and this canal, they're going to be our saviour, you know. Take us all the way to Manchester."

"Anywhere apart from Mortborough'll do fer me," replies Luke as they pass a 'Welcome to Walkley' sign. "Never comin' back 'ere again."

Brad asks, "What's in Manchester?"

"Massive refugee camp, or that's what I heard on the grapevine, at least. We'll be safe there, all of us."

"Maybe. But some of us don't just wanna be safe. Right, Jada? Some of us want revenge."

She folds her arms. "Justice, Brad. The truth. That's what I want. But I've got evidence. We've got Lena. We need to keep her alive, so she can expose those government crooks. Villeneuve, an' whoever else we uncover."

"Okay. I just feel like I wanna, ya know, *fight* 'em. When those black-suit bastards died before, it felt *good*."

"Well, it'll feel even better if we nail the people at the top, the string-pullers, not the grunts with guns at the bottom."

"She's right." Gould slows the motorboat. There's a submerged car in the water ahead, blocking half the way. "Go after the bastards in Westminster, not the stooges in uniform."

"What if some of us *do* want t' be safe?" Luke finds himself staring at a dead woman in the sunken vehicle. Most of her body is underwater; her head and shoulders are dry. "I got Connor t' think about."

Brad and Jada seem ready to argue, but they hold their tongues.

Gould interjects: "First thing you need is rest. All of you. Shit, I've just been sat in front of a TV, and *I* feel exhausted!"

Luke understands why the other two disagree with him. His friend Brad's lost the most important person in his life, and vengeance is probably the only thing keeping despair at bay. Jada is a truth-seeker to the core, and only a lobotomy or death will stop her.

So perhaps they will part ways. Safety for himself and Connor has to take precedence. *'N' what about Dad, Maddie 'n' Mason in Atherbury?*

Suddenly exhausted, Luke looks skywards and yawns. There are drones beneath the scattered clouds. Helicopters and two chemical-spewing aeroplanes, too.

Can we ever really be safe now? Even if we can, fer how long?

Printed in Great Britain
by Amazon